WE ARE FAMILY

ALSO BY LOUISE WALTERS

Mrs Sinclair's Suitcase

A Life Between Us

The Road to California

The Hermit

WE ARE FAMILY

Louise Walters

LWB

2024

Louise Walters Books

We Are Family
by Louise Walters
Copyright © Louise Walters 2024

The moral right of the author has been asserted according to the
Copyright, Designs and Patents Act 1988

All rights are reserved

A catalogue card for this book is available from the British Library
First produced and published in 2024 by Louise Walters Books

ISBN 9781739109561

Also available in e-book

Typeset in PTSerif by Louise Walters Books
Printed and bound in Great Britain by 4edge Ltd

louisewaltersbooks.co.uk
info@louisewaltersbooks.co.uk

Louise Walters Books
Northamptonshire
UK

For my friends

Tracy, Tessa, and Tricia

(not always seen, but always there)

WINTER

Shock!

Later, when she had stopped crying, she picked up the little white stick to check again that there were definitely two blue lines. There were. Not one, as she had hoped and expected. Two. Two was positive. Two was real. Two meant she had fallen at the last hurdle. Two was a great big YES when what she wanted was a small, quiet, of course-you're-not, don't-be-ridiculous, you're-too-grown-up-for-that, no. You're too peri-menopausal for that, damn it! Jennifer slumped on to her toilet seat and stared at her reflection in the huge floor-to-ceiling gilt bathroom mirror. She gazed into herself for a long time, looking beyond the make-up and professionally dyed jet-black hair, beyond the barely noticeable but confidence-boosting facelift she had undergone a few months ago.

She went downstairs and made strong coffee. Jake sniffed around her, his tail wagging. He was always pleased to see her. She sat at her kitchen island, Jake at her feet, and she ran through the situation in her clear and precise mind. These are the facts she considered, and this is the order she put them in:

Number one, she was pregnant.

Number two, she could not face another termination.

Number three, she could not face another loss.

Number four, in two days' time, on 14 November 2017, she would be forty-nine years old.

The Silk Champagne Teddy

(size ten)

Alison seated herself at the computer, and splashed coffee on to her brand new pink cashmere jumper.

'Bloody hell!' she said, dabbing at the coffee with a tissue. She grimaced and shook her head. She really must get on with the grocery shop. She wanted tomorrow evening as her delivery slot: it was the cheapest time to take delivery, and as Malcolm was always saying, *in times like these we must economise*. Malcolm and Alison had been married for twenty-two years. The *times like these* had existed throughout their marriage.

He was middle-aged (always had been), middle-height, and middle-intelligence. Alison wasn't sure if she still loved him. Of course, she was middle-aged too and possibly she always had been, just like Malcolm. Maybe that was why they'd been drawn to each other. Kindred middle-aged spirits.

The favourites list appeared on the screen, and Alison began the necessary ritual of clicking "add" against those items wanted again this week. She put a song on YouTube to break up the boredom. After some thought she chose 'We've Only Just Begun' by The Carpenters. Karen Carpenter's voice always soothed her and made her think of luxurious things, like silk, and excellent chocolate. It was a very middle-aged song.

Alison stared at the computer screen. What were Luxury Belgian Chocolates doing on her favourites list? She never bought supermarket chocolates. She always bought from Hotel Chocolat and never for herself. Alison frowned. Then her mind cleared.

Malcolm! He must have popped into the supermarket one evening after work to buy them for her. They were probably languishing on the back seat of his car, forgotten under his jacket and old sandwich wrappers and newspapers.

'Flowers?' said Alison, frowning harder.

It was a large bouquet, expensive at twenty pounds, including sunflowers and yellow gerbera and yellow tulips. Alison didn't like yellow, and Malcolm knew it.

Alison continued with her shop. And then one more alien item popped up on the list, and shattered her world.

'Oh my God!' said Alison.

She reached for the telephone and, with a shaking hand, punched in a familiar sequence of numbers. She felt an unwelcome hot flush creep up her body, sweat beginning to prickle on her legs, her back. It would have to happen *now*.

'Jennifer Sawyer,' announced the familiar, assured voice. If there was a crack in the voice, an unusual tremor, Alison didn't notice.

'Jennifer? It's Alison!'

'Ally? You all right? You sound agitated.'

'I am agitated. I've made a dreadful – *dreadful* – discovery.'

'Ethan's not gay, is he?' said Jennifer, who couldn't resist a joke. She knew full well Ethan wasn't gay.

'What? No! Don't be facetious. Ethan is not gay. It's Malcolm!'

'Malcolm's gay?'

5

'Jennifer! I do wish you'd be serious. Malcolm is not gay. He's the opposite of gay. He's having an affair. With a... woman.'

Silence.

'Are you still there?' said Alison.

'I'm still here. How do you know Malcolm is having an affair?'

Alison told her closest friend about the favourites list, the chocolates, and the bouquet. 'And if that wasn't enough,' Alison continued, 'I've now just found, on my favourites list, mind you, *my* list... a silk champagne teddy!'

'You mean like a bear holding a bottle of champagne or something?'

'No, you idiot! Listen to me. A silk teddy. In a champagne colourway! Size ten!' Alison knew she was barking down the telephone, but she no longer cared.

'Oh, I see. One of those clingy little numbers that looks fabulous with stockings and suspenders?' said Jennifer.

'Oh my God!' said Alison.

'But how do you know these things aren't for you, Ally?' asked Jennifer, hopefully.

'I just know. It's all wrong. Something is very wrong here.'

'Would you like me to come over?'

'Yes please.'

Jennifer arrived twenty minutes later, looking fabulous in a yellow trench coat. Alison admired the cut of the coat and wondered how much her friend had spent on it. Jennifer was fond of clothes and fond of buying them. But then, wouldn't Alison be the same if she could afford it? And it wasn't as if Jennifer wasn't generous. On their periodic shopping trips, Jennifer always bought her something lovely, to cheer her up. The pink cashmere jumper was the latest treat. Alison hoped the coffee stain didn't show.

'Let's have a look at the evidence, then,' said Jennifer, peeling off her coat and flinging it over the back of the sofa.

Alison showed her the offending items.

'The teddy thing is a bit cheap, isn't it?' said Jennifer, straightening up.

'What do you mean?'

'I doubt it's real silk, is what I mean,' said Jennifer, frowning at the screen.

'That's hardly relevant, is it?' said Alison.

'I suppose not. Anyway, he's a bloody fool!'

'For cheating on me?'

'For using the loyalty card. He's well and truly found out!'

Alison eyed her friend with derision. Jennifer shrugged.

'Thank you. Thank you so much, Jennifer.'

'For what?' said Jennifer.

'For your unstinting help and support.'

'Oh, come on, Ally. You've got to laugh.'

'Laugh at what? My husband having an affair? You might find that highly amusing, but I don't!'

'How do you really know these things aren't for you?'

'Because I hate yellow flowers. I'm sorry, but I don't like yellow, and you know that, and I haven't been a size ten since nineteen ninety-five. Besides, my husband never buys me... clothing. He never has. It's one of our unspoken rules. And I don't eat chocolate.'

'I see. Never? But I've seen you eat chocolate, haven't I? Many times.'

'I eat very good chocolate, in small amounts, very occasionally,' said Alison, reddening.

'Since when has an entire tin of Quality Street been classed as "a small amount"?' said Jennifer.

Alison recalled one regrettable occasion. She was pretty sure it was the occasion Jennifer was referring to.

'Don't be so judgemental,' Alison said.

'I'm not being judgemental. I just know fact from fiction. Look, Alison. Perhaps he just bought the wrong size teddy? It's quite flattering, isn't it? He still sees you as a size ten. He still finds you attractive. Or... or perhaps he is being... you know. Maybe he wants to spice things up between you? He's at that age. You could always take it back and change it. What's the occasion, anyway?'

'That's just it! Haven't you listened to a word I've said? There is no *occasion*. Our anniversary was in May, if you recall. Twenty-two years. That's the copper anniversary, apparently. We had a candle-lit dinner at Mario's, don't you remember? Christmas is still a month away. Malcolm buys his present for me on Christmas Eve, he always has done. No. These things are not for me. They're for another woman.'

'That's an awfully big conclusion to jump to,' said Jennifer, perching on Alison's coffee-coloured velour sofa.

'I don't know what other conclusion there can possibly be.' Alison slumped on to the sofa alongside her friend, and both women became lost in thought.

'You're a bit quiet,' said Alison at last. 'Are you all right?'

'Me? Oh, I'm fine. Just a bit of a headache today. Too much coffee I expect. I must detox again soon.'

Alison looked at Jennifer. How she envied the perfect make-up, the still-quite-fresh skin, the apparent lack of grey hairs, the slim figure unscarred by pregnancy and childbirth; the sophisticated, single existence. Jennifer had been married once, to Patrick. Jennifer had lost herself to Patrick, and had more or less lost touch with Alison for as long as the marriage had lasted, which was ten years. Jennifer had done very well out of it. Patrick had given her a "huge lump sum", and one of his houses, the best one. Jennifer had resided there ever since, queen of her castle, her black Honda LS standing like a horse-

and-barouche on the gravel drive, her garden well-tended by a (young, handsome) man who came in twice a week (Jennifer did not touch soil); and the handsome man's (young, pretty) wife also came in to clean Jennifer's house, twice a week. Jennifer paid them both generously. The wife also cooked sometimes, helping Jennifer out with her entertaining. Jennifer was a generous host and always had good wine in the house; sometimes sharing a bottle with Alison.

'Do you think it's his secretary?' said Alison. 'Cliché by numbers I know, but that's Malcolm all over, isn't it? He has little imagination.'

'Come off it! I met her at your Christmas party last year and she's no more a size ten than—'

'Than I am?'

'Well. Yes. Sorry.'

'If he's in love with her he probably sees her as a size ten. Men don't recognise sizes, that's a well known fact.'

'Exactly! But nobody could mistake her for a size ten. And she had BO.'

'Don't be so cruel.'

'It's the truth!'

'Yes, you're right. I remember. It can't be her. Oh, Jennifer, who is it? What's going on?'

'Nothing's going on. I promise you.'

'If you weren't such a good friend I'd even suspect you, you know.'

'Me?'

'Yes, you. You've got a bit of a track record with men.'

'I have not had sex with your husband!'

'You've had sex with other husbands,' said Alison.

'Yes. I have, but not with yours. It's unthinkable.'

'He's not good enough for you, I suppose?' said Alison.

'He's not good enough for me, no, since you ask. Like you

said, he has no imagination. But that's not the reason. He's your husband and you are my best friend.'

'I didn't say no imagination. I said little imagination.'

'Whatever.'

'So who is this cow?' said Alison.

'I don't think there is a cow. I think there's an innocent explanation.' Jennifer took Alison's hand. 'Malcolm loves you. There's no doubting that. He has such a... *soft* look in his eyes when he looks at you.'

'Really?'

The front door opened and slammed shut.

'Is that...?' said Jennifer.

'Ethan. Back from college. In here, love!' called Alison.

Jennifer stood up.

'Hi, Mum,' said Ethan, as he entered the room. 'What's for tea— oh!'

'Hello, Ethan,' said Jennifer.

'Hi, Aunty Jennifer. I didn't expect to see you. Is everything all right?'

'We're okay, Ethan. Nothing to worry about,' said Alison.

Ethan's eyes widened as he caught sight of the computer screen and registered the picture of the silk champagne teddy, size ten. He looked at his mother's strained face. He didn't look at Jennifer.

'Your mum thinks your dad is having an affair,' said Jennifer. 'He appears to have purchased all sorts of... *cheap* items on line, using the loyalty card of course, because he didn't *think* and now he's found out. What do you make of that, young Ethan?'

Alison started to cry. Ethan, a kind and affectionate young man, put his arm around his mum's shoulders. Although he was very red in the face, he seemed composed.

'It's not Dad,' said Ethan. 'It's me.'

'You?' said both women, their eyes pinned on him like lionesses watching over the most precious cub in the pride. Then Jennifer muttered, 'As I suspected...'

'Yes. Me. I've got the key fob card that links to your account, Mum, remember? I bought these things... for my... girlfriend. For Helena. From college. You know, Mum.'

'But... but... she's a *friend*... you're just a boy! Oh, Ethan!' Alison stared at her son with a mixture of shock and relief.

'I'm eighteen, remember? An adult? I do adult things. You can chuck my Lego out now. OK? Just not the Death Star.'

Alison slowly smiled through her tears. Ethan went off into the kitchen to make a sandwich. Jennifer announced that she was going home. It was her birthday tomorrow, if they had remembered, and she had things to do. Alison said of course she had remembered. She had posted a card. She hadn't been sure if she would be seeing her... but would take her out for dinner one evening soon... Jennifer blew a kiss goodbye.

Alison finished her grocery shop and reflected. Malcolm – dependable, loyal Malcolm – was not having an affair after all, not even with Jennifer. Especially not with Jennifer. Of course he wasn't. But Ethan... Ethan had grown up and she'd failed to notice. He was right, the Lego would have to go. She'd get Malcolm to clamber up into the loft at the weekend and chuck it away, along with the Action Man stuff and the cuddly Mr Tickle that Ethan had begged her to buy one rainy Saturday at the market, long, long ago. You couldn't keep things forever.

She hoped they were being careful, Ethan and Helena. Something else... what was it? Helena and Ethan *having sex*. She shuddered. Helena. A nice girl. A bit... brash, perhaps. Mousy and plain. Perhaps a little over-confident. She'd only met her twice. Sweetly plump. That was it! Helena, a size ten? No. No, she was not. Maybe the choice of size was a deliberate ploy, designed to avoid offence, as Jennifer had suggested. To flatter. Men and their hopeless muddled ways. But the fact remained: Helena, like Alison, like Malcolm's secretary, was not a size ten.

Denial

On her birthday, Jennifer rang Simon at eleven o'clock. She knew he took a coffee break around then, would see it was her number, and would pick up. He always did.

'Hello, you sexy lady.'

She didn't want to agonise over the words, so she said, 'Hello, Simon. I'm with child.'

'Hang on…' muffled words, noises, a chair scraping. He was sending somebody out of his office. 'OK. You mean you're up the duff?'

'Yes.'

'And you're… forty… three?'

'Forty-nine, Simon. Today, actually.'

'And?'

'And I'm letting you know.'

'What does it have to do with me?'

'What do you think?'

'It can't be mine.'

'I beg your pardon?'

'It can't be mine.'

Should she hang up, or continue to be insulted? 'Are you calling me a slut or a liar?'

'I shouldn't wonder if you're not a smidge of both, old girl.'

'It takes one to know one.'

'Slut or liar?'

'Both.'

'Ooh, touché, young Jennifer.'

Simon was forty-four. An investment banker, and a former friend of Patrick's. She had always quite fancied him from afar; and a couple of months ago when he had rang her out of the blue, she had asked him out for a drink. They had slept together half a dozen times. Simon was married. They hadn't used protection, hadn't discussed it.

After the unsatisfactory call with Simon, she did another test. Still positive. Of course. She was also getting a vague feeling of nausea. She must act quickly before this thing got a hold. She rang her GP surgery, and got an appointment (somebody had cancelled) that afternoon.

It was a new doctor who she hadn't seen before. Young, good-looking, brown-skinned, with a deep voice. But she put that to one side. No more young men. No more young*er* men. No more men.

'Take a seat. What can I do for you?'

'I'm pregnant.'

Was that a flicker of surprise? A small movement. She looked young for her years, but of course her notes were on the screen so he would know exactly how old she was.

'As you can see, I'm no spring chicken.'

'Is this your first pregnancy, Miss Sawyer?'

'Jennifer, please. No. Everything should be on my notes.'

'Yes, of course... let's have a look. Do you have a family?'

'No. I'm divorced. It's just me and my dog, Jake. I had an ill-advised fling, Doctor...' she studied the lanyard '...Doctor Henry, and I find myself with child at the age of forty-nine. What you might call the eleventh hour.'

'You may know there are risks associated with pregnancy at your age.'

'I want an abortion. I've decided. No question.'

'I see. Are you sure you're pregnant?'

'Yes. Two positive tests on two different days, and I'm starting to feel sick. My period is late although the last three or four have been a little irregular.'

'That's probably perimenopause.'

Probably. Did she really need a funky, sexy, slim, twenty-something, cool, brown-skinned, doctor-dude to tell her that? Life was packed with irony. Irony upon irony. 'It probably is,' she said.

'I can refer you to a clinic. They should be able to see you within a few days. They will probably do an ultrasound to confirm the pregnancy and if it's as early as you think it is, the termination will be simple. Any chance the pregnancy is further along than you estimate?'

'No. No, it's not possible, Doctor Henry. I know exactly when this child was conceived.'

'I see. I'll make the referral and you should hear from them within a week or so.'

'Thank you.'

The ultrasound at the clinic would confirm her dates. She made it four weeks, so she would have conceived about two weeks ago. She'd had to google it. She had forgotten all of this stuff. She couldn't quite recall the date of her last period. They had become... more than irregular. Erratic. Chaotic. A bit like her "love" life. Her last night with Simon had been just over a fortnight ago. At least she knew that. She wanted the "simple" termination, the pills. Not the other type.

She should have been more careful. But here she was, caught out, at last. Caught out *again*. Last chance. No. She was having a termination, no matter what. *No matter what, Jennifer.* She'd done it before, she could do it again. She would have to face the loss.

Meeting

1982

Alison stood alone among the maelstrom and wondered what on earth she should do or where she should go. Boys spat on the ground and swore and shouted at each other in harsh adolescent voices, ignoring her entirely. Girls giggled, stared, and looked her up and down. Older kids, sixth formers and not in uniform, seemed impossibly huge to her. Her old school didn't have a sixth form. The smells were of course familiar – sweat, chewing gum, gymnasium – and Alison screwed up her nose and pretended to rearrange things in her bag. She felt tears welling up and wanted desperately not to cry, not on this day, not among all these new kids.

'Hey!'

Alison looked up. A gang of four girls, all taller than her, all prettier, much prettier, stood in front of her. They looked her up and down too. Two of them whispered about her pleated skirt, pointing at it. Alison knew it was horribly old-fashioned. Her mum didn't seem to understand this.

'Are you new?' asked one of the girls, who had masses of blonde curls.

'Yes,' said Alison, looking at the girls' feet. She knew, from the way they were dressed, the way they spoke, and the way they were laughing at her, that this was the In Crowd. They were no different to the In Crowd at her old school. These replicas would probably make her life just as much hell here too. Well done, Mum and Dad, yet another sideways step. Didn't they get it? No. They didn't.

'What year?' said Blonde Curls. Her skirt, unpleated, was short. She had slim taut legs, tanned. She was probably good at hockey.

'Third year. I... moved here in the summer holidays. It's my first day and I don't know where to go,' said Alison, and she burst into tears.

'Oh my God!' said Blonde Curls, backing away as if Alison's tears were contagious. Then: 'You're a bit short for a third year, aren't you?'

'I can't— help— my height,' said Alison, quietly, forcing herself to stop crying. She thought nobody had heard.

'Let's go,' demanded Blonde Curls, tossing her head and turning away from the specimen that was Alison. Two of the other girls followed her as she walked away, but the fourth girl lingered.

'No, you can't help your height,' said the girl. 'But nice things come in small packages. Here,' and she offered Alison a piece of scrunched-up toilet tissue. 'It's clean.'

Alison blew her nose and afterwards looked up at the girl. She had long sleek black hair, neatly tied back in a high pony tail, and tanned skin, and deep brown eyes. She was impossibly pretty. She smiled at Alison.

'Take no notice of her,' the pretty girl said, indicating the disappearing Blonde Curls. 'I'll show you where to go. I think we'll try the staff room. You are expected, aren't you?'

'Yes. My name's down and all that. My mum and me came in yesterday to have a look round, when there were just teachers here. But it looks different today.'

'Come on, then,' and the girl stalked off, Alison following her. When they reached the staff room door, the girl collared a young male teacher, whose face became very pink while talking to her. He agreed to take over with Alison and show her where to go.

'Thanks, sir,' said the girl, and she rested her hand on Alison's shoulder. 'You're in very safe hands with Mr Coburn,' she said, and she looked at the teacher with a meaning Alison couldn't fathom. He blushed even pinker. The tall girl walked away, swaying her slim hips and tossing her long ponytail. Then she stopped, and looked over her shoulder.

'By the way, what's your name?' she called.

'Alison Baker. Thank you,' said Alison, trying to sound grateful.

'I'm Jennifer Sawyer. See you around, Ally Pally.'

Malcolm

1982

Like her, Malcolm Timmins came from another school, also to escape bullying. Three weeks into the new school year, he was put into her form, seated behind her. Soon they were sharing geography homework. He had a quiet voice, curly blonde-brown hair; *kind* hair, if that was possible. A friendly way with him: sincere, and earnest, and... what was it? He was gentle. Homely. That was the closest word. He was like a cosy couch.

The In Crowd were smitten by Alison-and-Malcolm. They were cuties! The third year's Romeo-and-Juliet. The square Romeo-and-Juliet. The uncool Romeo-and-Juliet.

Jennifer gave Alison all manner of advice. About sex, about birth control, about being careful.

'Like you were?' said Alison. They were sitting on a bench in the quad. Boys were spitting, swearing, shouting. But not Malcolm. Never Malcolm. He was a gentleman, even then.

Jennifer was unfazed. Alison understood by then that Jennifer was never fazed. Jennifer shrugged. 'Yeah. Well. I won't be making that mistake again. I'm on the pill now.'

'You mean you...?'

'Of course I did. My mum took me. My dad doesn't know.'

'Are you all right?'

'Course. I've got my O levels to think about.'

'O levels can be done later in life.'

'So can being a mum. Anyway, Al-the-Pal, have you and Malc-the-Talc done it yet?'

'No!'

'What do you mean, "No!"?'

'We're waiting.'

'For what? A bus? Christmas? To die?'

'Don't be stupid. We're being sensible.'

'Sod being sensible. You live once.'

'I don't want to end up in a clinic with my mum.'

'No, you don't, so get on the pill and start living. You're fifteen. Not a kid.'

'I'm fourteen!'

The following Saturday afternoon, in her bedroom, while her mum and dad watched *Grandstand* downstairs, Alison almost did it with Malcolm. Neither of them knew quite what to do; both of them knew they were too young. So they were careful. They were sensible. Malcolm surprised her, as he always would, although sometimes, across the years, it would be too easy to forget that. 'Let's just wait,' he said. And Alison sat up, relieved. And they waited.

Happy Birthday

Ethan reclined naked on the king size bed. He took a Luxury Belgian Chocolate from the opened box on the bed next to him. She stood before him, resplendent in the "silk" champagne teddy, size ten, and flesh-coloured stockings and suspenders.

'How do I look?' she said, swaying towards him and lowering her body on to his. She kissed him.

'Delicious,' said Ethan. 'Happy birthday.'

'Oh, young Ethan, you are a silly, silly boy. Now, tell me. What have you done with that loyalty fob?' She swung her black hair back from her face and smiled at him.

'I've chopped it up into lots of little bits and thrown it away, *Aunty* Jennifer, just like you told me to.' (Of course, he hadn't).

'Good. You can leave all the buying to me in future,' said Jennifer, who could be very generous. 'On no account is your mother to get wind of this. Us. How could you be such a stupid Ethan?'

God, what a young idiot he was. But he wouldn't make that mistake again, she'd make sure of that. She'd been... seeing... Ethan for about three months. On and off. He'd called round to her house, on some errand for his mum. She couldn't recall what. One minute they were in the kitchen talking, simple small talk, the next she'd told him how grown up he was these days. She'd rubbed his arm, in an aunt-like fashion, then not in an aunt-like fashion. She had lingered on his muscles, then had touched his other arm, feeling the muscles there too.

'Oh my, young Ethan.'

The next thing they were kissing, and before she knew it they were in her bedroom having sex. He kept coming back for more, and she kept letting him.

She knew it couldn't last, and she guessed he knew he was being used. There was no love. Any that existed was the distant aunt-ish love he'd grown up with. *Aunty* Jennifer: presents on his birthday and at Christmas when he was a kid, then money in a rude birthday card once he'd turned sixteen, a bottle of vodka at Christmas. (She tried to be a cool aunt). An aunt who cared enough, but was not prepared to get emotionally dirty.

But tonight, she would forget about... everything. Her troubles. Being *in trouble*. This would be the last time, and tomorrow she would tell him so. She would not make this mistake again. It was... it wasn't *right*. And every time they had sex, a vision of a shocked Alison, a disgusted Alison, loomed in her mind, and it was difficult to shake it.

Neither she nor Ethan would be heart-broken. It wouldn't be a wrench for either of them. Ethan had his girl at college. Helena. There would be other girls too. Many of them. Hopefully. He was quite good-looking. Didn't bear much resemblance to either of his parents, although he had a hint of Alison about his eyes, his mouth. He looked nothing like Malcolm. Yes, hearts would be broken, but not hers.

Jennifer was good at compartmentalising. It was possible to put emotions in a box, and shut the lid on them. Tonight would be fun, and tomorrow it would be over, and tomorrow she would tell him it was over. She would ring him, maybe even text him. She would become a "proper" aunt again.

Scandal!

1983

When the scandal broke, Mr Coburn was sacked and everybody knew what had happened. *Everybody.* By then, in the fifth year, Jennifer was the undisputed queen bee. Even the sixth formers bowed to her superiority.

Alison felt it wasn't entirely Mr Coburn's fault. He was young – twenty-four, as they later found out – and Jennifer by then was sixteen. He should have known better, of course. He was the grown up. She had already had that abortion, a fact which still both terrified and electrified Alison. The drama of it, the pure... *adventure*, as she naively thought of it. And now, poor pink-faced Mr Coburn, a vapid-but-adequate teacher of history, sacked. Disgraced. It was wrong, what they had done; Alison knew that. Mr Coburn had behaved very badly. So had Jennifer, Alison supposed. But she would stand by her friend. Jennifer had taken her under her wing since her first day at this school, and that had saved her skin. Always looking out for her at break times. Warning away the bullies in Alison's year when they threatened her. Alison's status as Jennifer Sawyer's pet elevated her to the In Crowd's outer ring, which meant she was one of their favourites who would occasionally have their notice and "friendship" bestowed upon her.

Jennifer bumped into Alison one lunchtime after Mr Coburn had left.

'Hey, Ally Pally!' she called, and left her group, beckoning Alison towards her. Alison looked at her friends, who rolled their eyes, and shrugged, and drifted away. Jennifer's friends laughed, but drifted away too, leaving the two girls alone in the centre of the school's "quad". Really it was just a worn and muddy patch of grass with some spindly trees planted in the middle and benches against the buildings all around. Jennifer hooked some second years off a bench, and she and Alison sat on it.

'I'm in trouble, Ally Pally,' said Jennifer.

'What sort of trouble?'

'Trouble. In trouble.'

Alison felt her eyes widening, in horror and intrigue. 'Who?' she whispered, already guessing.

'Mr Coburn, of course.'

'You went *all the way*?'

'Why d'you think he was sacked? Of course we bloody did! It was good too. Older men know what to do. Know what I mean? But now look at me.'

Alison looked. Jennifer looked the same as ever. Gorgeous. The bell rang. 'But you're on the pill.'

Jennifer shrugged. 'Didn't work.'

'What are you going to do about it?'

'What do you think? I'm sixteen.'

'Oh Jennifer, not ag—'

'See you later, Ally.'

A week later, Jennifer told Alison that she had "started" and there was no baby. What a relief. No need to go back to that clinic. No need to tell anybody, especially Mr Coburn.

Alison's Wedding

1995

The wedding list was coming together. Mum fussed about neighbours, former neighbours, neighbours' neighbours. The list was becoming too big.

'Have we included all the friends you wanted?' Mum asked, again. Alison wished her mother would relax. It was supposed to be fun, all of this. Wedding planning. Mother and daughter preparing for the big day. Dad kept out of it. *Let the women get on with organising.* He paid for things.

'Yes.'

In truth, Alison had few friends. A couple of work colleagues and their grumpy husbands. One girl from university with whom she had remained in touch. Jennifer, of course, her long-standing but on-and-off friend, and her only bridesmaid. Jennifer had a new boyfriend: Patrick. Patrick with black hair like Jennifer's, with deep brown eyes like Jennifer's, with expensive tastes like Jennifer's. Alison had met him twice and felt looked-down-upon on both occasions. He said things he thought were funny, but were merely arrogant and rude.

Jennifer picked Alison up to go for another dress-fitting. There was a month to go until the wedding. They were in Jennifer's car, which smelled of lemons.

'Aren't I by rights the matron of honour?' said Jennifer. 'I'm older than you. I can't therefore be your bridesmaid.'

'Oh, who cares? It's not like you're being asked to be a flower girl. And you are not a matron. You're only twenty-five.'

'Twenty-six. You're twenty-five.'

'Oh yes.'

'Does it have to be purple? The frock?'

'Yes. Purple-and-ivory is the theme.'

'But you know I don't do purple. It's hid— it's not my colour.'

'It's *my* colour, Jennifer. Watch that lorry... what's he *doing*? That's the point. It's my day, and my choice.'

'What about red?' said Jennifer, confidently negotiating the lorry.

'No.'

'Green? Blue? A nice pale blue would be lovely.'

'It's a bit late in the day to start whining about your dress. Why didn't you say something before?'

'I didn't like to.'

'So why now? Don't you understand the stress involved in planning a wedding?'

'Of course I do. It's aged you about six years in six months.'

'Oh, thank you.'

'I was joking. But is it all worth it? All this stress? For fucking *Malcolm*?'

'If you don't want to be my bridesmaid, matron, whatever, just say so.'

'I'm not sure that I do.'

Alison, already annoyed by an argument with her mother earlier that morning, burst into tears.

Jennifer hastened to console. 'Of course I'll be your bridesmaid. And I'll wear purple. You're right, it is your day, your colour choices. Malcolm's a good man. Boring, but good.

I like him, very much. He's also a remarkably lucky man. I am sorry, Alison.'

'You say that.'

'I mean it. Tell you what, once we're done I'll buy us lunch somewhere nice.'

'I'm only eating salads at the moment.'

'Then I know just the place.'

Jennifer's Wedding

1999

There was to be no purple at Jennifer's wedding. Not a hint. Ivory, yes, a wedding wasn't a wedding without ivory; but with yellow. That was the theme. And the right yellow, not cheap and sunshiny, nor feeble like a primrose. In between. Yellow roses. A beautiful bouquet. A June wedding, with all the flowers in the world to choose from.

And for Jennifer, all the men in the world to choose from. Many of them at her feet. She had *it*, she knew she had *it*, and she hoped *it* would never leave her, and abandon her to her fate. Patrick might be a terrible fate. As she walked down the aisle (no bridesmaids, just her and the beautiful yellow roses) towards Patrick, she forced herself to see the ££. There was nothing else to see. Patrick was handsome in his plastic way. Patrick could give her an awful lot of what she wanted. Things. A home. A car. He didn't want children. *They'd get in the way*. In the way of what? She didn't ask, because she agreed with him. Kids always got in the way. She had been "seeing" Patrick for four years, not always exclusively. Then one day, out of the blue, he'd got down on one knee and asked her to be his wife.

She hadn't seen Alison for a while. Months. Years, really. It wasn't that they were avoiding each other. Jennifer wanted to avoid Malcolm, or so she told herself. Malc-the-Talc, as she'd always called him. What a boring man. Why on earth had Ally Pally married him? Teenage sweethearts. No other man, Jennifer suspected, ever. Never. Well, apart from... never mind. Alison's contentment baffled her. Jennifer had sent a wedding invitation – ceremony, reception, and evening-do – and received a prompt polite acceptance card. Their friendship wasn't strained, exactly. Muted, perhaps. Was that the right word? Over the years it had peaked and troughed, they had been in and out of each other's lives, dramas, moments. Sometimes it didn't feel like a friendship at all; at other times Jennifer knew Alison was her best friend; the very best friend she would ever have; her only friend.

She knew Alison was hurt not to have been asked to be matron of honour, nor a bridesmaid, and she knew Alison wouldn't be ameliorated. Their friendship would have to settle itself around this new slight. But it was Jennifer's day. Her choices. Just like Alison's wedding day had been governed by her choices. It was natural. Jennifer chose to have no matron of honour, no bridesmaids, no flower girls.

After the ceremony, during the photographs, when Jennifer noticed Alison's bulging abdomen, and studied closely her fleshed-out face, and Malcolm's beaming pride, Jennifer felt... what? Betrayed. Why hadn't she told her? She must have been pregnant for some time. Jennifer felt, strangely, insulted – Alison had allowed *Malcolm* to get her into that state? – and more than that. The feeling she couldn't acknowledge, the emotion she hated to feel above all others, and indeed rarely felt. It wasn't allowed. It was weak and pathetic. A terrible emotion. And – Alison had chosen not to tell her she was pregnant. She'd had no idea. Perhaps that was poetic. But why hadn't she told her?

She knew she would distance herself from Alison. Their

lives had diverted so much since leaving school. Alison, content with her little husband, little life, little (large) baby-bump. It was sad to see. Jennifer accepted Alison's cool congratulations with grace, and leaned in for a kiss on the cheek from Malcolm.

Jennifer didn't mention the baby bump. And Alison knew Jennifer was deliberately ignoring the obvious, of course she did, and something opened up between them, a gulf. It would be bridged, one day, Jennifer trusted that, but she didn't know when. Not for a year or seven. Get that bloody baby out and born and growing up! Alison would be insufferable, doting on it, showing it off, expecting the entire world to love and adore her ugly little sprog. The offspring of Alison and Malcolm, the most boring couple in the world.

Oh, that terrible emotion.

Jennifer's Honeymoon

1999

Patrick's truest colours emerged for Jennifer three days after the wedding, on honeymoon in Paris. They were in a restaurant, eating oysters, drinking champagne, and the waiter was good-looking. Jennifer may have flirted with him. Patrick said she did. Jennifer denied it. She wasn't sure. She was being friendly. She was happy. A pretty – no, beautiful – thirty-year-old English woman on her honeymoon, in Paris, and, well, that woman is going to sparkle. She had married a handsome, generous, wealthy man. They were in a classy restaurant, and they were delirious and warm from sex and excitement. Beautiful women get noticed, especially in Paris, and of course sexy young waiters are noticed right back. So perhaps she smiled too long, or too much; maybe she flicked her hair once too often. She didn't simper, she never did that. Flirting was too serious for simpering.

Back in the hotel room, as soon as the door was closed behind them, Patrick's smile became a sneer.

'What the hell were you playing at in the restaurant?'

'What do you mean?'

'The waiter!'

Jennifer, shocked. Patrick trembling.

'Don't be so ridiculous,' she said.

Two strides, and a ringing slap, and her life really did change forever. 'Don't you ever, *ever*, call me ridiculous. Got it?'

Jennifer righted herself, held her hand to her face. 'Yes. Why are you being like this?'

'Being like what? You're my wife. How do you think it made me feel?'

'Patrick... I'm sorry.'

'So you should be. Look, forget it. It doesn't matter. But I need to know I can trust you.'

'You can trust me.'

'Good. Now go and get ready for bed.'

Ethan

1999

'She's a *fucking bitch*, Malcolm!'

Malcolm and the harassed-but-calm midwife exchanged understanding glances. Twelve hours into labour, that hot August day, and Alison was high on Pethidine and pain. She never swore. Until now.

And for this she would swear. She wasn't a prude. She was giving birth, wasn't she? Proof that she wasn't a prude. But why the pain? Why did it have to hurt so much? Why couldn't she share the pain with Malcolm? Why... Oh God... these fucking... Oh God!... These waves...! *Float away, just float away...*

Better. Gone. And he just stands there, gormless, like a guppy fish. No wonder Jennifer hasn't been around. Doesn't even know she's in labour. They haven't spoke in months. They haven't spok*en* in months. Grammar. Slipping... another one! Oh no! Malcolm! Do something. He places a wet flannel on her forehead.

'Fuck off, Malcolm! This baby needs to get out of me NOW!' Did she shriek it aloud? Or just in her head? It was lonely in her head. Pain in her head, in her body, everywhere, overwhelming pain and it was all Malcolm's fault.

Malcolm took away the flannel.

'This is your fucking fault!'

Malcolm and the midwife exchanged further understanding glances.

Then: she was a mother. Magically, suddenly, and everything changed, her life came into sharp focus. Her baby, red-faced, so ugly if he – *he?!* – wasn't so beautiful. He was covered in something that looked like cottage cheese. He was sort-of crying. Exclaiming? He smelled divine. The midwife was smiling, and Malcolm was crying, and then so was she, great racking sobs of joy and relief. It was over. The torture was over. And her new life had begun. She counted his ten perfect little fingers. He suckled at her breast, latched on, no problem. The midwife sloped off and came back with hot sweet tea, one each for her and Malcolm. The midwife examined the baby while they drank. She weighed him, pronounced him a healthy baby boy.

When he was handed back to her, dressed in a little blue crocheted hat, wrapped in blankets, and before she had to rise up off the birthing bed and get into the shower, Alison knew four things:

Number one, her little boy would be called Ethan. Malcolm would just have to deal with that.

Number two, she would never, ever, go through this pain again. Malcolm was going to have to deal with that too.

Number three, she would never go through that awful nausea again.

Number four, Jennifer didn't know what she was missing.

Missing Alison

2008

Jennifer *did* know what she was missing: her freedom, her safety, her self-respect. Patrick had stripped her of everything. He'd not slapped her again. No, she had gathered her strength and told him that she would not tolerate that. Never again. But he lied, whined, cajoled, intimidated, frustrated, gas-lit, and emotionally blackmailed. He showered her with gifts, and Jennifer settled. She *settled*. It wasn't a bad settle. He knew that she was prepared to stick up for herself. He tried to explain his jealousy (that terrible emotion) and she forgave him. For the sake of the houses, the cars, the holidays, the clothes, the high-end make-up, and now their puppy, Jake-slash-Samson, a German shepherd who worshipped Jennifer and, at best, tolerated Patrick.

She knew he was sleeping with another woman; women. Perhaps he slapped them around instead of her. It was possible; probable, even. And it kept her safe, so she turned that all-seeing blind eye. Selfish? Possibly.

She saw Alison's baby photos on Facebook. She "liked" them, and sent over an expensive hamper of baby things and new mum things. Later, she received an invitation to the christening, which she declined. No. She could not do that. She

36

would have to disappoint Alison and Malcolm. She didn't want Patrick anywhere near that baby.

Alison became even more distant after the christening. No doubt she was upset that Jennifer and Patrick had been "unable" to attend. Friendship, all those years, since their schooldays, reduced to birthday cards and Christmas cards and an occasional phone call (usually made my Alison). Alison was busy with the baby, Jennifer told herself. A new mum, finding her place in the world. So what if she was over-weight, over-wrought, and not much fun? Their friendship would handle it. They had been through quite a lot together, either on the playing fields or on the side-lines, shouting encouragement and support, since 1982. Alison never really had been *fun* anyway. Too serious, the most earnest person Jennifer knew. Straight as a die. Perhaps it was surprising that their friendship had lasted as long as it had. And perhaps now it was finally petering out. People came and went, didn't they? Alison could be... boring. That was the truth of it. A boring friend who you kept purely to remind you how your own life could turn out if you made shit decisions.

How ironic was that?

It was her idea to get Jake-slash-Samson, and it was done cynically. She wanted protection. A dog would be perfect. She "persuaded" Patrick (using several saucy outfits). In the end Patrick believed it to be his idea, and he insisted on the name: Samson. Jennifer allowed it. She got the puppy, and she worked hard to train him. In her mind he was Jake, would always be Jake, but to the world he was Samson.

Jennifer believed it to be her idea that she didn't want to maintain her friendship with Alison. Other, albeit distant, friendships went too. All her friends were Patrick's friends, his work colleagues; they saw his family (occasionally); rarely hers. Not that she had much family, with Mum long dead and Dad in a home. No siblings. No extended family. It couldn't have been more perfect for Patrick.

Missing Jennifer

2008

Alison awoke one morning with a hankering for Jennifer's company. She wasn't sure where it had come from, or why. It has been at least two years, by her reckoning, since their last phone call; longer, even. The cards still arrived, still got sent. That was something: a sign, wasn't it? Of a continuing if distanced friendship? And that gorgeous hamper when Ethan was born. She'd not forgotten that. She had telephoned Jennifer to thank her, and Patrick had picked up. She didn't like him. He wouldn't pass her over to Jennifer, seemingly wanting to chat to her instead. How was Malc? (Fine, thank you.) Was Alison going back to work? (No.) Wasn't it time Jennifer had a baby too? (That might not be her thing, Patrick.) *Didn't they discuss it before they married?*

Patrick had been part of the reason she'd stopped calling. He was a moron, and there was something more… something almost sinister about him. When she'd mentioned it to Malcolm he'd brushed it aside. 'Patrick? He's all right, isn't he? Her type.'

Of course she could see the material advantages in being married to Patrick. The house was out of this world, the cars impressive, the holidays exotic and expensive.

But, and Alison had always prided herself on her intuition, Patrick was not a good man. She also prided herself on her ability to see the truth in people; that simple unadulterated stream, right at the core of people, that ran through them and could not be altered. Jennifer wasn't a *good* woman… she was fun, charming, attractive, good company if you liked a sardonic humour (which Alison did, despite not having a sardonic bone in her body) but it was these very attractions that made her bad. Still, she was her friend, her only true friend, the friend she had known the longest, and she owed her a call, despite the huge slight of Ethan's christening. It wouldn't have hurt Jennifer, would it, to have turned up? To think she had even been considering asking Jennifer and Patrick to be godparents. Malcolm, despite his assertion that Patrick was "all right", had manged to talk her out of that one. Instead Malcolm's cousin was Ethan's godmother. A woman they barely saw. Then she had emigrated to New Zealand. Alison often wondered if this was why Jennifer had turned down the christening invitation: because she had not been trusted with the godmother role. Not that it truly meant anything. Alison had perhaps recovered from her disappointment at not being Jennifer's matron of honour. So maybe now they were quits.

Ethan had been at school these past four years and Alison felt empty because of it. Empty in her heart. She was struggling to accept her baby was a child. Not even a toddler now. She had stuck to her guns. Ethan, like her, and like Malcolm, indeed like Jennifer, would be an only child. She simply could not bear to go through that again. No. Never. Besides, she was sterilised, and Malcolm was snipped. She had insisted.

'Jennifer? It's Alison.'

'Ally Pally!'

'It's been ages since we spoke.'

'I'm shit at maths, but I make it around two years.'

'Yes, two years. I'm sorry.'

'Not your fault. How's Malc?'

'He's all right.'

'Still at the same place?'

'Eleven years and counting.'

'Staying power, that one.'

'And how is Patrick?'

Did she imagine it, or was there an un-Jennifer-like intake of breath? Hesitancy?

'Patrick's fine.'

'And is he still at the same place?'

'Of course he is, you idiot. He owns it.'

'Yes. Of course. Sorry. Baby brain.'

'Ethan's not a baby. Is he at school yet?'

'Of course. He's nine.'

'Right, so no baby-brain bullshit.'

'Jennifer, honestly, you are so—'

'I'm right, is what you were about to say. I'm always right.'

'Nobody is always right, Jennifer.'

'I know. I was kidding. And how are you doing?'

'I thought you'd never ask. I'm fine. A bit bored.'

'You going back to work?'

'Not sure.'

'A part-time job might be good for you.'

'That's what Malcolm says. Or I could volunteer, he says. In a charity shop.'

'Yes, you could.'

'I know you've never set foot inside one, but I like them.'

'I have been in one. I dropped off a load of old clothes last year in the Princess Louise Hospital shop. So there.'

'I'm impressed.'

'It smelled disgusting.'

Alison laughed, a big loud laugh she couldn't hold in. 'Maybe you *are* always right,' she said.

'We have a new addition,' said Jennifer.

'Really?!'

'Don't get too excited. I have a dog. He's a beautiful boy.'

'Oh. I didn't think you were a dog person.'

'I didn't think so either, but... you know.'

Alison didn't know, but she forged ahead with the standard questions. The dog was a German shepherd, and his name was Jake, although Patrick insisted on calling him Samson. Alison felt something wasn't quite right in the whole dog scenario. It wasn't like Jennifer to want, let alone own, a dog. She was so clean, so house-proud, so particular. But she must have her reasons, Alison supposed.

They made a vague arrangement to meet for coffee. But somehow, it took another year to achieve it. Ethan caught chicken pox... then Christmas... then Malcolm and Alison had the flu... later, in March, Alison started volunteering in the Princess Louise shop, two days a week. But she never saw Jennifer in there. Ethan had some bother in school. He was bullied, a bit, although neither Alison or Malcolm would ever use that word. They secretly each blamed themselves. And Alison wished Ethan could find his version of Jennifer.

Which he did. They put him in a new primary school, after the May half term break, and on his first day he came home full of talk about a boy named Reuben with whom he was already best friends. Reuben had an older brother and a twin sister at the same school. Reuben's friends were their friends. There was no more trouble, after that.

Finally, a coffee date was arranged. Alison and Jennifer were rather nervous about it, although nether would admit it, even to themselves.

Coffee

2009

Alison arrived at the coffee shop first, which was customary. She found a decent table near the back but not too close to the toilets. She texted Jennifer: *I'm here x,* and then she waited.

She studied Jennifer as she approached the table. She was thin. Even for her, she who had never been fat. Pale too, her usual honey-cream complexion – aided by good make-up, of course – not quite present; and was her black hair a little more drab than she'd ever seen it? No greys though. Good sign. She was still taking care of herself. But something was off. Perhaps she could have been a better friend over the last few years. More attentive. But Ethan was all-consuming. Jennifer would understand that, surely? Even though she had no kids, she surely could see what it was to have them?

They embraced, warmly. They ordered coffee (Americano for Jennifer, cappuccino frappe for Alison), and they made small talk waiting for their drinks to arrive. After the waitress had kindly brought over their order, they caught each other trying to sneak in an appraising look at the other. They laughed, and the ice melted, just like the cubes in Alison's frappe.

'I'm sorry, Jennifer,' said Alison.

'For what?'

'I'm not sure. Something… is there something wrong?'

'In what sense?'

'Are you… ill, for instance?'

'No.'

'Are you… tired?'

'Yes.'

'Tired because…?'

'Just tired.'

They weren't going to get anywhere, Alison could tell. Defensive Jennifer was in full flow.

'Would you like to see some photos of Ethan? I brought some to show you. I know you see the ones I put on Facebook, but that's not the same.'

Well, it was the same, but Jennifer made the right noises at the right times in the right places, even cooing at one point. It was quite sweet, in that peculiar Jennifer way. She didn't like children, and made no bones about it, so it was clear she was making an effort.

Alison carefully put the photos back into her handbag. The coffees were almost finished. Jennifer put her hand on Alison's. It was unexpected. Jennifer was trembling. Her hand felt unnaturally cold.

'What is it, Jennifer?' Alison said, putting her other hand over Jennifer's.

Jennifer was trying not to cry. Then Alison sensed that internal shutter crashing down, and Jennifer withdrew her hand, and leaned back in her chair. 'Nothing,' she said. 'I'm tired, that's all. Genuinely.'

They chatted some more, about nothing much, and ordered a second coffee each; then they arranged to meet again soon. Then Alison had to go; she was standing in for another volunteer that afternoon in the charity shop.

'Take care, Jennifer,' she said, and Jennifer assured her that she would. Alison watched anxiously as Jennifer walked away. She was definitely thinner than she'd ever seen her. But not healthy-thin. Something was wrong, Alison knew in her heart.

They didn't see each other for another two years.

Separation

2009

He sauntered into the kitchen, whistling, as he often did. It had always annoyed her, but now, ten years into the marriage, it made her want to scream. And ten years was enough, she had finally decided last night, on the eve of their anniversary. No more.

He had another woman; semi-serious, this time, Jennifer suspected. Rebecca. Worked at his business. Not a secretary, something else. Didn't matter what. Rebecca was the latest, but Patrick had never been faithful. Jennifer had known this from the early months of their marriage.

Neither was Jennifer faithful, of course. But Patrick didn't know; or didn't notice, more accurately. The last one had been the electrician who'd worked on their house. He had a girlfriend, but it "wasn't serious" (except it was, because he was married within a few weeks of his one day stand with Jennifer).

'Would you stop that whistling?' she said. She fed Jake. Jake ate with chompy slobbery enthusiasm.

'I like whistling.'

'I don't like to hear it.'

'Do one, Jennifer.'

'You'd like that, wouldn't you? Rebecca could move in.'

He put down his coffee. He glared at her. She raised her eyebrows.

'You're a cow,' he said. Jake looked up from his food bowl.

'Whatever, Patrick. It's over.'

'What's over?'

'Our marriage.'

'That's for me to decide.'

'Is it really.'

'Really. I own this house, and the London house, and the cottage. You own nothing and you would be nothing without me. You have nothing to your name.'

Jake growled. Patrick took a step away, and picked up his coffee. He was red-faced.

'I've spoken with a solicitor,' said Jennifer. 'Not yours, of course. I have my own now.'

'And?'

'I have a right to half of all you have. It makes no difference if the houses are only in your name. So I want this one. And an allowance. That's all. I don't want the other properties. I want you to move out, hand the deed over to me, and go live your life with Rebecca, or whoever might follow, and leave me to live mine.'

'You want a divorce?'

'Eventually. Separation, for now, is fine.'

'How long have you been planning this?'

'A year or so.'

'My god.'

She'd been putting money away, "small" amounts (she was aware of how well-off they were) from their joint account. He'd never noticed. She had savings, her own secret bank account. She had always used cash for shopping, preferred it. He had never commented on the cash withdrawals.

'You're an even bigger bitch than I thought.'

Jake barked, growled, moved towards Patrick, who was so angry he didn't seem to notice.

'Get the hell out of my house!' Patrick snarled, and he reached out, and for the second time in their marriage, the second time in a decade, he slapped her. Hard, with the back of his hand, so that she stumbled, fell, hit her face on the corner of the kitchen island. She cried out.

It all happened so quickly. Patrick's coffee cup smashed on to the floor. He screamed. Jennifer stood up, watching, in shock, but powerless to stop it. Jake took a bite out of Patrick's hand, the hand that had slapped Jennifer. He was going to bite it off.

She collected herself. 'Jake! No!' He stopped, and whimpered, and crept to her side. He licked her hand that she put down to calm him. Patrick cried, pathetic sobs that failed to move either Jennifer or Jake.

'I'll call an ambulance,' Jennifer said, and she did. Patrick wrapped his hand in a tea towel. Jennifer sent Jake out into the garden with a dog biscuit.

'That bastard of a dog is gonna be put down,' said Patrick. 'Make no mistake.'

'No, he's not. I'm going to tell the ambulance crew what happened. The dog defended me because you were beating me up. Want that to be known? Far and wide?'

Patrick clutched his hand. He was deathly pale.

'So, we were having a row. It upset the dog. He bit you. Defending me. Unfortunate. After you're done at the hospital, you can go to the London flat or wherever you choose, and make your life there. And I will live here, without you. You can get your stuff as and when. I'll keep Jake out of your way.'

'Jake?'

'That's his real name.'

'You really are a bitch,' Patrick said.

'Sometimes you have to be a bitch, Patrick. You of all people should know that. And if you ever, ever, hurt me again, if you get in my way, I'll set Jake on you and I won't call him off, and I'll tell everybody, and I mean everybody, how you've treated me. The first person I'll tell is poor Rebecca.'

The ambulance, blue lights flashing, swept on to the wide gravel drive. Jennifer panicked then, wondering how on earth she would explain away the huge angry darkening bump on her temple, which was now throbbing. But explain it away she would.

Rose at the Clinic

It was the same clinic, the same building, from all those years ago. Different staff, of course, but all fulfilling the same role. *This Morning* airing on the wall-mounted TV. Dog-eared home and decor magazines on the teak oval coffee table. A phone ringing. A woman at the reception desk – "Sally" – tapping on a keyboard.

The nurse's lanyard announced her name as Rose, but Jennifer knew the drill. Fake first names (only) here. This was just a new Rose.

Rose asked a few questions, and then prepared for the ultrasound. She smeared the gel on Jennifer's belly. The monitor was turned away from Jennifer, of course. For some women it must be the only way to cope with this part. Not seeing it. Rose moved the probe around, digging in quite hard.

'I make you nine weeks pregnant,' she announced after a bit of staring at the screen, and clicking of keys, and huffing and puffing.

Was she asthmatic? That was all Jennifer could think.

Then: 'Nine?' Jennifer asked. Had to ask. It couldn't be right.

'Yes. Just over.'

'I made it four,' Jennifer said. 'Are you sure it's not four?'

'I'm sure. Nine weeks.'

'Can I see it, please?'

'If you would like to, yes.'

No, she bloody well would not like to. Nine weeks? 'Yes please.' She stared at the monitor. Rose took hold of her hand. 'Is there anything wrong with it?' Jennifer asked, hoping against hope.

Rose, it turned out, was the wisest woman Jennifer had ever met. She handed her a clump of tissues. She cleaned the gel from her belly, and helped her to sit up. She said most women asked if there is anything wrong. To be told there is alleviates the pain, and the guilt, in those who felt it. Only natural. There was nothing wrong, as far as Rose could tell. Early days, but all was looking as it should be for a foetus of nine weeks and two days gestation.

Gestation. What a word.

Go home, Rose said. Sleep on it. 'Give me a call tomorrow. Make this decision with your heart, Jennifer. At your stage in life, it's only the heart that matters.'

Not strictly true, but Jennifer knew what she meant. Rose talked about the risks. Down's syndrome. Other things. All the things that would mean a termination would be a perfectly reasonable course of action at four weeks, as Jennifer had thought. But nine weeks? That was different. As Rose prattled on, kindly, Jennifer did her calculations. Nine weeks would mean it would be... the baby would be born in... June? July? A summer baby. And something deep inside of her closed, or opened; she wasn't sure which. She thanked Rose and made to leave. She had to get out of there.

'Ring me tomorrow,' said Rose.

Rose at the Clinic II

'Hello, you're speaking to Rose.'

'Hi Rose, it's Jennifer. You saw me in the clinic yesterday.'

'Yes, of course. How are you?'

'I'm fine, actually. I want to thank you for your kindness.'

'Oh...'

'Your compassion and common sense were just what I needed.'

'I'm glad to hear it, Jennifer.'

'I'm going to have a baby. I'm going to be a mum. At long last.'

'Oh, Jennifer! That is wonderful.'

'I can't do it, Rose, you see. I can't do it again.'

'I... see. Of course not.'

'No. I mean, I can't *give up* another one.'

'I understand. A termination is never an easy option.'

'But I had a child. I don't talk about her. Ever.'

'I'm sorry to hear that.'

'I'm not maternal. Never have been. I don't like kids. I thought I would grow to, back then. But as the pregnancy progressed I knew I couldn't do it. So towards the end I chose adoption and on the day she was born I said goodbye to her.'

'How old were you?'

'Twenty-five. Not that young. But not old enough, for me.'

'It was probably a selfless act, Jennifer.'

'Maybe. Sel*fish*, I always think. They let me name her, so I chose Marnie. The prettiest name I could think of. Nobody knows about her. Not even my best friend.'

'You chose a beautiful name.'

'It was a clean-break adoption. Closed. No contact. I didn't want to hear how she was growing. Couldn't bear to. I made up my mind it was nothing more than a very late termination, you see? That was how I framed it to myself. Justified it, I should probably say. That's what it was, to me.'

'That was your decision to make. Perhaps the right decision.'

'So you see I can't do either of those things again. I won't have another abortion, and I won't give this baby up for adoption. So I'm stuck with it.'

'It does rather look that way. If it's any consolation older women tend to make brilliant mothers. I should know. My mother was forty-five when she had me.'

'Brave woman.'

'You're right, she was brave, and so are you. I know this is a huge step.'

'It is. Massive. I'm terrified.'

'Of course you are. But you'll be OK.'

'I've never even changed a nappy.'

Rose chuckled. 'After day one, you'll feel like you've been doing it for years. Promise.'

But she could have been changing nappies in her life, couldn't she? If not her own baby's, then Alison's baby's. She could have been a better friend, a better "aunt". She could have been involved.

'Thank you, Rose. Thanks for talking. But can I check? Is it definitely nine weeks? Not four?'

'Nine weeks and two days. Everything pointed to that.'

'I see. Thanks, Rose.'
'Good luck, Jennifer. Fare well.'
'I'll try.'

Bye Bye Baby

She wondered why she had ever suspected Malcolm of having an affair. Or a fling. Or a one-night stand. He wasn't! He never would. He wouldn't know how to do these things. Jennifer was right about that. So she felt guilty now for even thinking it. It wasn't in his blood. It wasn't in hers. Well. Maybe it had been, once, in hers. And literally only once. But a long time ago, and forgotten.

Ethan's childhood treasures were stacked and packed in the hall, ready to go to the charity shop. Not his *baby* baby stuff, though: his first pair of Clark's shoes, the knitted pram blanket her mum had made, his little sailor suit (3 to 6 months, Mothercare). No, those things, along with a whole tub full of other baby stuff, she was keeping. She had "been through" the entire lot, looking at everything, refolding, cleaning out the tub, putting it all away again neatly, adding a sprinkling of lavender essential oil, and it was firmly ensconced back in its rightful corner of their small loft.

It had been a busy week. She couldn't part with any of her son's stuff without careful consideration. Malcolm had urged her to just get rid; Ethan said more or less the same thing. The Lego Death Star was still all he wanted to keep. It had been gathering dust in his bedroom for years. Everything else could go; and he had even gone through his room himself over the weekend, adding to the stacks in the hallway. She sadly contemplated the big pile of Goosebumps books. Alison had gradually snaffled those for him when she'd volunteered in the Princess Louise charity shop. She'd paid for them, of course: donating 50p for each title she had wanted for Ethan. He'd been a big reader, until he'd discovered gaming, aged twelve. Then that was that. Now he only read what he had to for his college course.

And now he had a girlfriend, and he was officially an adult. Old enough to have sex. The thought was uncomfortable. Was she a prude? Perhaps. She and Malcolm... well, not for a while. Months. Had it been over a year now? She'd gone off it. Malcolm was patient. Understanding. "Under her thumb", as Jennifer had once put it in her insensitive manner.

So perhaps it hadn't been so crazy to have suspected Malcolm of having it off with somebody else. Men were men. Even Malcolm. And slappers were slappers, she thought uncharitably. Then she felt guilty. Jennifer would never sleep with Malcolm. And Alison knew, beyond any doubt, that Malcolm would never sleep with Jennifer. Even if he wanted to. But if Malcolm was... if he was more like Jennifer's type, would she want to sleep with him? If he looked like that hunky young gardener of hers? Alison couldn't honestly answer that. Jennifer had a thing for husbands. That was just the husbands Alison knew about. Goodness knew how many men she had slept with over the years. Too many. And where had it got her, truthfully?

Alison sighed, and stood up. She'd have a coffee, then load some of the stuff into her car, and take it to her old charity shop. She knew how grateful they would be.

It was time to accept the end of an era. Ethan's childhood consigned to memories, photographs, never-watched videos on memory sticks, a tub of stuff in the loft. Would she want to start all over again? No! Once was enough, one child was enough. Malcolm had wanted more. Perhaps she should have had another, a brother or sister for Ethan. Only is lonely? She knew that, Malcolm did too. But the nausea she had suffered for four solid months, the hospitalisations... she had never been thinner, before or since, than she had been for the first half of her pregnancy. One of her life's craziest ironies. She just could not go through that again nor the pain of childbirth, although that memory had faded over the years. The memory of the nausea however had not faded, and she still feared feeling sick.

Alison picked up the cuddly, tatty, faded, matted, Mr Tickle. *Please, Mum? Please? He's my absloot favourite!* She took Mr Tickle upstairs and stuffed him in the bottom of her wardrobe.

Nervous

Thirteen weeks. A few days over thirteen weeks. No sign of a miscarriage. Not a drop of blood. She had hoped... sort-of-hoped... that nature would take its course. And it had. But it seemed that nature wanted her to go ahead with the pregnancy. Three whole months come and gone. Perhaps it was time now to contact the midwife at the GP surgery. Perhaps she should have done so already.

The sickness was OK. Not so much morning sickness as evening. Had Alison suffered with sickness? Somehow, she thought she had... surely she had once mentioned having to go to hospital, and having painful injections to stop her throwing up. They had been rather out of touch at that time... honestly, Jennifer hadn't been the best of friends. She should have tried harder, kept in contact, not been so... well... that word. *That* emotion.

A cup of ginger tea seemed to work, about eight o'clock in the evening. Her bedtime. Eight! She hadn't been to bed at eight since she was seven years old. But she was so tired... and she slept in most mornings until at least eight. Twelve hours of solid sleep. On waking, she would plump up her pillows and read, or listen to the radio, before indulging in a long hot shower. How on earth did women who worked *cope*?

She was ready for Christmas. She was off to Alison's gaff for dinner on Christmas Day, taking up the kind invitation that she had accepted for the past six or seven years, since her dad had died. Lunch was served at two, on the dot. Then Malcolm, and Alison, insisted on watching the queen at three o'clock. Followed by dessert, which was always a stodgy homemade Christmas pudding. Charades. The tray game. Then around six o'clock Jennifer usually walked home, belly full of food and booze. Malcolm, the gallant gent that he was, always walked her to her door. She always felt tipsy after her Christmas Day at Alison's.

But not this year. They would wonder why. She would have to tell them. Make up a father... may as well stick to the Simon-as-father idea that she'd originally presumed to be the case. Ethan would be there, with his fat girlfriend Helena. No, Jennifer! Bad word! Not fat. "Generously proportioned". Alison always tutted if the word fat was used, of anybody.

Jennifer wasn't yet fat. But it was coming, and her waistbands were almost too tight now. This was going to be a huge challenge. She had always been slim, almost for all of her life. She recalled the first pregnancy, the despair of her huge belly, accusing and rotund as she lay in the bath. She had felt exhausted and, if she had been able to admit it, at that time, terrified. Alison was right; Jennifer would not be fat. She would be generously proportioned. And it would be temporary. The saving grace.

Ethan. He must never know. He was already gutted that she had ended their dalliance. He had been... not angry, not upset... disappointed? He wasn't a clever lad, so she hoped he would simply accept that he was not the father. Of course, he was. He was the only possibility, but she would never let on, so she had a story all good to go if he challenged her: *I sleep around, Ethan. Did you think you were the only one? I'm sorry if I gave you that impression. We used condoms, remember? Anyway, the timings don't work. I know who the father of this baby is, and it's not you.*

That would work. She'd lie about the due date, just in case he did some digging of his own. Put it back a couple of weeks, throw him off the scent. He really wasn't a clever lad. They did use condoms. One had split. Ethan had worried. Jennifer hadn't worried. She had assumed, at her stage in life, that she was out of the danger zone. She didn't bother going to the chemist for a morning after pill. What a momentous decision that had turned out to be. But she didn't want Ethan to work it all out.

She sat at her kitchen island and wrapped her gifts. A very nice single malt whisky for Malcolm; a fancy vodka for Ethan; a bottle of Angel perfume for Alison; a large box of Hotel Chocolat chocolates for all of them. She had even bought a last-minute gift for Helena: a large Soap and Glory set. Let it never be said that Jennifer Sawyer was tight with gifts.

Jake snoozed at her feet. The house was silent, save for the rustling of wrapping paper, the zip of sticky tape. This silence would end in the summer. It was, despite all the fears, misgivings, and secrets, an exciting thought.

How would she tell them? When? Over dinner? After the queen? She was oddly nervous. She rarely felt nervous. Perhaps it was only natural. She had no idea, none at all, how they would react.

Shock! II

Helena was quite a spiteful girl, thought Jennifer, observing her over the dinner table. The jealous type. Thought a lot of herself. But what really did she have to think so highly of? It wasn't her looks, although they weren't great... but Jennifer wasn't focused on those. Had Helena been a nicer person, her looks would be nicer too... Jennifer was vain but not so vain as to be blind to this sort of thing. Inner beauty was always obvious by its presence or absence. No, it was Helena's personality. Or lack of it. What on earth did Ethan *see* in her? No wonder he'd— best not go there. Their dalliance, regrettable, stupid, must be forgotten. Nobody need ever know, as long as Ethan kept it to himself. In that she would simply have to trust.

Malcolm carefully, slowly, carved the turkey, during which time the vegetables cooled. Alison popped them into the microwave to warm them up. Jennifer's appetite was large today. She found herself becoming impatient to start eating. This wasn't like her, she who had always enjoyed food, but had never been greedy, because she enjoyed being slim too. But there was no point in worrying about her figure now. It was going to be wrested from her. She looked coolly at Helena; chubby (another word Not Allowed by Alison), and loading her plate with probably two or three more roast potatoes than she strictly needed. *Stop it, Jennifer*, she admonished herself. *Don't be a bitch.* Was Helena a size eighteen? Perhaps twenty? "Big". The kind of sizes she would need to start wearing in a couple of months... Jennifer took the proffered dish of roast potatoes from Helena and put two on her plate. She passed the bowl to Ethan. She then accepted one of the bowls of vegetables from Malcolm and piled lots of those on to her plate.

When she had arrived in her car, Alison had asked why. Jennifer had made some excuse, and Alison hadn't really been listening. 'If I do end up drinking too much I'll walk home and come back and fetch it in the morning,' Jennifer had placated. Thank goodness it was raining heavily, providing a plausible excuse for driving.

'Da-da!' cried Alison, emerging from the kitchen brandishing a bottle of Prosecco.

'No, thank you,' said Jennifer, placing her hand over her glass.

Alison, Malcolm, and Ethan all stared at her. Helena looked from one to the other, uncertain.

'I'm... well, I'm thinking of giving up drinking. That's why I brought the car, you see. So I don't drink. That and the rain.' She glanced at Alison, who had raised one eyebrow. She had always been able to do that.

'Giving up wine, Jennifer?' said Alison. She poured her own glass, and finally sat down to eat. 'That's not like you.'

'I know.'

'What's brought this on?' said Malcolm, a forkful of turkey hovering before him.

'A health kick, Malc, actually. I had a... an MOT at the doctors and I was told I am exceeding my alcohol limit, regularly, and I should cut down.' It was sort-of-true. She did drink too much. Regularly.

'But it's Christmas Day!' said Alison. 'Just have one glass.'

'No. Thank you. Do you have any sparkling water?'

Alison shot her a look. Then she got up, and went back into the kitchen.

'Sorry!' called Jennifer.

Helena regarded her thoughtfully. Jennifer ignored her.

'Here we are,' said Alison, plonking a bottle of supermarket own-brand fizzy water in front of Jennifer.

'Alison?' said Malcolm, embarrassed. To his credit, Jennifer thought. He was always the politest person in the room.

'Well... look, I'm sorry, Jennifer. I'm just rather surprised, that's all.'

Oh god. Should she just tell them, now? It would save any awkwardness later, and it would shut Alison up. Why was she being so weird? *Alison wasn't being weird. Let's get this over with.* She unscrewed the bottle of fizzy water and poured some into her wine glass. They all carried on eating. She could feel Helena still analysing her. Jennifer put down her knife and fork.

'Actually, I have something to... I have some news.'

They all looked at her. Not unkindly. Apart from Helena. Jennifer now doubted that the girl had a kind bone in her body. What *did* Ethan see in her?

'I'm expecting a baby.'

An intake of breath from Ethan. Eagle-eyed Helena looking sharply at him. Alison open-mouthed. Malcolm with another forkful of turkey poised to be eaten.

'But you're forty-nine!' cried Alison.

'Yes, I am.' Was this all Alison could come up with? It was reasonable, Jennifer had to concede. A reasonable thought, in the circumstances. She felt Helena scrutinise her with increased zeal. Jennifer's age was clearly news to her.

'Jennifer,' said Malcolm, picking up his glass and holding it up. 'Congratulations to you. That's what my wife meant to say.'

The silence was long and excruciating.

'I'm sorry, I'm just... shocked,' said Alison. 'I'm totally shocked. What are you going to do?'

'How do you mean?' said Jennifer, and took a sip of her fizzy water. She stared back at the haughty-looking Helena, who looked down at her rapidly-depleting plate.

'Well...' said Alison.

'I'm going to be a mother, Alison. I'm going to raise a child.'

'Of course you are,' said Malcolm. 'What lovely news on Christmas Day.'

Helena said, 'Congratulations!' and reached for the bowl of Yorkshire puddings.

Ethan said, 'Now we know why you brought your car,' and took a huge gulp of Prosecco.

Jennifer glanced at him, smiled, and murmured, 'That's right.' He was very red in the face.

Malcolm said, 'More wine, Alison?'

Alison, holding out her glass for a refill, burst into tears.

Tears of joy, of course, she later claimed, as she opened her present from Jennifer. They had watched the queen. Malcolm was asnooze at his usual end of the sofa. Helena and Ethan were in the kitchen, where Ethan was unloading and reloading the dishwasher.

'Oh! Angel perfume! Thank you, Jennifer.'

'Don't act so surprised. I buy it for you every year.'

'I know. I just forget.'

'No you don't.'

Jennifer opened her gift from Alison. A bottle of Hendricks gin.

'I'm sorry,' said Alison. 'I had no idea—'

'Of course you didn't. Why would you? Neither did I until a month ago. I'll save it for July.'

'Why didn't you tell us earlier?'

'Twelve weeks and all that. I'm thirteen weeks now.'

'Of course. I understand.' Then, anxiously, 'Much sickness?'

'No. I'm fortunate. I feel a bit sick in the evenings. Haven't been sick though.'

'Oh, Jennifer, that is such a relief. I was so bad with Ethan.'

'Didn't you end up in hospital?'

'Four damned times!'

'You poor thing.'

'All forgotten now. Well, sort of. I dread stomach bugs. It takes me right back to it. Never felt so ill in all my life.'

'Is that why...?'

'Yes. Of course. Never again. And too late now. I'm amazed that you have managed it! You're older than me.'

'I suspect I won't menstruate ever again. It really was an eleventh hour thing.'

'May I ask...?'

'Some bloke I've known for a while. Nobody special. I'm going it alone. Not even going to let him know. I don't need a man to mess this up for me.'

'Oh, Jennifer... are you sure?'

'Sure of what?'

'You want to go it alone?'

'Yes. And I have no choice, really. He's... in a relationship.' Jennifer knew that to lie successfully, you must stay as close to the truth as possible. 'And he's younger than me.'

The "snoozing" Malcolm uttered a small cough. Jennifer had guessed all along that he was listening. Alison passed the tin of Quality Street to Jennifer.

'Oh, Jennifer, really?' said Alison. 'How much younger?'

'Quite a bit younger. No chocs for me, thanks.'

'Dear oh dear,' Alison said.

'Ally,' said Jennifer, 'are you going to bring me a bowl of

your Christmas pudding, or do I have to go and prepare it myself?'

'How much younger? You know, specifically?'

'I don't want to talk about it, Alison. I'm just looking to the future, you know?'

'The pudding will be ready in a few minutes. I'm boiling it on the stove. I'm doing it properly.'

Of course she was.

'Fifteen years or so younger,' said Jennifer. Malcolm coughed again, and pretended to wake up.

'I'll go and see to the pudding,' said Alison.

'Lovely!' said Malcolm.

Aftershocks

'Is she your real aunt, though?' asked Helena, moving out of Ethan's way so he could reach up to the cupboard to put away the wine glasses from Christmas dinner. Mum had got new, clean, glasses out for the "dessert wine" to go with the Christmas pudding, which was steaming gently on the hob.

'No. She's my mum's oldest friend. They met at school.'

'How old is she, again?'

'She was forty-nine, I think, in November.'

'Old then. Can you even have a baby at that age?'

'It would seem so, yes.'

'She fancies herself a bit, doesn't she?'

'What do you mean?'

'Like my mum would say, she's pleased with what she sees in the mirror. She's attractive. For her age.'

'Yeah. Probs. I hadn't really noticed.'

'Liar, liar, pants on fire. You went very red in the face when she told us she was going to have a baby.'

'Did I?'

'Yes. Jealous, are we?'

'Of what?'

'The guy who's done the deed.'

'No! I was a bit surprised. Like you said, she's a bit old.'

'Isn't she just.'

Jennifer went home, zooming off up their street in her sleek Honda, at around five o'clock. She was tired. She had to get back for Jake. 'It was a lovely day, Alison, thanks so much for having me. And cheers, Malc. Enjoy that whisky.'

He poured himself a glass, on the rocks. Alison poured a Baileys, also on the rocks. Ethan and Helena had disappeared upstairs. Alison turned up the television a couple of notches.

'Strange woman, your friend,' said Malcolm, stretching his legs.

'How so?'

'Pregnant? At her age? After all those years of not wanting children?'

'Yes. I hear you, Malcolm. Aren't you happy for her?'

'Yes, if she's happy, we're happy, aren't we?'

'Of course. You know, I think it will be the making of her.'

'Who's the daddy? That's the million dollar question.'

'I don't suppose it's anybody we know.'

'Shouldn't think so. She tends to move in quite exalted circles.'

'Not always.'

'Ooh. Tell me more.'

'I've long suspected she's... having a fling with... that gardener chap of hers.'

'Really?'

'It would fit with the age difference she claimed, wouldn't it? He must be thirty-something.'

'He's married, isn't he?'

'Yes.'

'Still up to her old tricks, then.'

'Of course she is. Leopards never change their spots.'

'Don't you mean cougars?'

'Malcolm!'

Aunty J, plz tell me I'm not the father. Am I? And delete this text too plz.

You are not the father. No worries on that score.

Thnx for letting me know. I have been worried.

No problem.

Who is the father?

MYOB.

Fair enough. Deleting all these texts now.

Ditto.

'Din-dins, Jake. Here you are, handsome. Merry Christmas.'

Jake tucked into his bowl of Pedigree Chum. Jennifer sat at her kitchen island with a mug of peppermint tea. She'd eaten too much at Alison's today. Peppermint tea would help.

She'd slipped into joggers once she'd got home. With trepidation she realised that even these would not fit her in a few weeks. 'What a mess, eh, Jake?'

Jake looked up from his bowl, decided no response was required, and continued his slurpy eating.

She didn't like lying, but she had no choice where Ethan was concerned. He must never, ever, know that her baby was his. Malc must never know. Ally must never know.

Jake looked up at her. His deep brown eyes seemed to say, 'What if the baby looks like Ethan?'

'Shut up and eat up, Jake. There's a good boy. Then we'll go for a little walk.' Jennifer yawned, stretched. Jake eyed her closely. 'Then I'm going to bed. Join me?'

Shock! III

Why Ethan wanted this part-time job, Alison couldn't imagine. Or couldn't work out. Malcolm gave him a generous-enough allowance every month. They bought his books and other study items.

Ethan popped upstairs to get ready for his interview. He came down a few minutes later in a nice clean shirt and a pair of his dad's trousers. Malcolm had gained very little weight over the years.

'You'll do,' said Alison. 'Good luck.'

'Hope you get it,' said Helena, almost sneering. She had been hanging around all morning.

Ethan kissed them both quickly and he was gone.

'Cup of coffee?' said Alison to Helena.

'Oh, yes please. Do you have any more of those nice biscuits we had last time?'

Helena was on her third biscuit. Alison made a point of picking up the packet and scrunching it closed. What she should have done, she now realised, was put three or four on a tea plate and bring that through from the kitchen. Helena was a generously proportioned girl with an appetite to match. Nothing wrong with that. But these were Malcolm's favourite biscuits and had been bought with him in mind. Not Helena.

Alison wondered again why Ethan was looking for a job. She may as well ask Helena.

'Oh,' said Helena, glancing at the now closed biscuit packet, 'I think it's to save for a holiday. For him and me. In July. Once college is over. Before we have to get proper jobs.'

'Oh... I see. Where are you going?'

'Not sure yet. Tenerife, maybe.'

'You like the sun.'

'Yeah.'

'And are you going to get a part-time job too?'

'No.'

'Oh. Are your parents going to pay for your share?'

'No.'

I see. Ethan's paying for both of you, is he? A bit lazy... perhaps Jennifer was right about her. 'Well, to help you both out we'll give Ethan some birthday money early.'

'Sound.'

'Ethan is a generous young man, you know. He gets it from his father.'

'Yeah.' Helena finished her coffee, and put the empty mug down on the tray.

'Of course, you know that. He bought you all those lovely things for your birthday in November.' Oh! Should she have mentioned it? She didn't want Helena to think she was a snooper.

'October. Yeah. I've used up all the bubble bath. Must get some more.'

'Bubble bath? That too?' *Hang on— October?*

'A body lotion to go with it. L'Occitane isn't cheap.'

'L'Occitane?'

'You've seen the shop in town, haven't you?'

'Yes, Helena, I have. What about the flowers?'

'What flowers?'

'The yellow bouquet,' Alison said quietly.

'I didn't get any flowers for my birthday.'

'Oh? Oh! Silly me. I'm getting confused. They came up on my supermarket favourites list, but it was Malcolm. They were a leaving gift for somebody at his work. I remember now.'

She wasn't the liar that Jennifer was, but it wasn't a bad effort. Helena smiled. Said nothing. Until, 'Couldn't have another of those biscuits, could I?'

Who the *hell* were the flowers for then? The chocolates? The silk champagne teddy?!

Ethan had got back from his interview, looking positive. He would hear about the job within a week. Alison offered to make tea (pizza, chips, salad) and the two youngsters had sloped off upstairs to Ethan's room.

Alison sat at her computer in the lounge. She was examining her favourites list. She was reminded that the teddy was a size ten. And Helena, with her appetite for Malcolm's favourite biscuits (she had taken two more, not one), was still not a size ten. It was likely she never had been, and never would be. And her birthday was in October. Not November. Those things had not been for Helena's birthday. But perhaps she had just assumed that? That must be it! They were just generous gifts for his girlfriend bought by her generous son. Out of love and affection. But... wouldn't Helena have said something? Wouldn't she have remembered the yellow bouquet? Birthday or not?

No. It was no use. Ethan had lied to her. He was lying to Helena, probably. He must be. He must have another girl. On the quiet. Goodness! She hadn't raised her son to be a philanderer. She'd have to speak to Malcolm about it.

Speaking to Malcolm About It

Her chance to speak to Malcolm came the following evening. Ethan left the house after tea to meet Helena and go to the cinema. Alison washed up, tidied the kitchen, and made hot drinks: builder's tea for Malcolm, chamomile tea for her. It always seemed to settle her mind.

'I'm worried about Ethan,' she said, sitting beside Malcolm. He was flicking through the TV channels.

'Why?'

'I think he's two-timing Helena.'

'Really?' He stopped flicking through the channels.

'Yes.'

'You can't blame him, I suppose.'

'Malcolm!'

'Well...'

'Don't be so cruel.'

'There's something about that girl I don't much like.'

'She is quite... greedy. But that's not really the point. Ethan isn't being fair to her.'

'What makes you think all this, then?' He took a slow sip of his tea. He had always been calm and measured.

She told him about the items on her favourites list. She told him that she had discussed it with Jennifer. She didn't tell him she had suspected him of having an affair. Because she hadn't, really, deep down, and Jennifer had made her realise her suspicions were ridiculous. She told him about her chat with Helena yesterday.

'I see,' said Malcolm.

'Do you think he's seeing somebody else?'

'Sounds like he might be.'

'Should we ask him about it?'

'Good lord, no. Alison. Think about it. He'd be embarrassed. So would we.'

'I suppose so. But what if he isn't being... sensible? He might catch something.'

'Well, yes, he might, but that's his look out.'

'Malcolm!'

'He is a young adult, love. Leave him be.'

'You and I have never two-timed.'

'I know, but we come from an older generation, don't we?'

'We're Gen X, Malcolm, not baby boomers!'

But they were, really, baby boomers. Older than their almost-fifty years. Always had been. So there was that gap between them and Ethan, that lack of communication, sometimes. Like now. Alison took sips of her chamomile tea. 'Should we say nothing, then?' she asked.

Malcolm had resumed channel hopping. 'We should say nothing,' he said.

The Silk Champagne Teddy II

Alison arrived at Jennifer's "mansion" (as she and Malcolm always referred to it) dead on eleven o'clock, the time she had arranged yesterday via text. They hadn't seen each other for a couple of weeks. Alison had popped into town first to buy a gift for Jennifer. She'd found herself drawn to L'Occitane. There she had bought some beautiful-smelling hand cream. Jennifer was inordinately proud of her hands, and took great pains to look after them.

Hence she had a gardener, who Alison greeted warmly as she got out of her car. What was his name? Something short, snappy, "vaguely sexy" as Jennifer had once said. But possibly she had been talking about the man himself, not his name.

'Morning!' she said, locking the car.

'All right, Alison?'

'Yes, I'm fine, thanks. Visiting the mother-to-be. Brought her something nice.' She held up the yellow L'Occitane bag. He nodded. He *was* vaguely sexy. Well, rather obviously sexy, really. He was wearing combats and a tight-fitting charcoal T-shirt. Was he the father of Jennifer's child? He certainly wasn't acting like he might be... but she wouldn't put anything past Jennifer. She turned to the front door, and rang the bell.

*

Jake sniffed around her with his usual lack of interest. He had grown used to her, Alison supposed, over the years.

'For you!' said Alison, and she put the bag on the kitchen island. Jennifer peeped inside after she'd brought their drinks to the island – coffee for Alison, ginger tea for her. She had "gone off" coffee weeks ago, she explained. She didn't drink normal tea, never had. She sat opposite Alison and took the hand cream from the bag. 'Thanks, Ally. That's gorgeous. You shouldn't have.'

'It's important to pamper yourself.'

'Oh, I do, don't worry! Baths every night now. I'm loving my baths.'

'That sounds lovely. What's your gardener's name again? I said hello to him when I arrived... but I can't for the life of me recall his name. He remembered mine.'

'Scott.'

'That's it. Scott.' *Vaguely sexy* indeed. The name suited the man.

'He's not the father, Alison. OK?'

Alison felt her face turn red. 'I just... I wondered. He is quite... attractive.'

'He's also married to a very nice woman, and he's a fantastic gardener and handyman, and she's a great cleaner, and a decent cook, and I need her. Kimberley. I'm not going to screw that up. By screwing him. OK?'

'Yes, all right. You don't need to be crude.'

Jennifer ignored the remark and offered Alison some of the L'Occitane hand cream.

'Ethan's got a Saturday job,' said Alison as she gently rubbed her hands together. 'In McDonald's.'

'Has he? Doing what?'

'He's "on fries", he tells me. He's worked just two days and he's already saying "fries" is the worst job there.'

'Good for him.'

'He and Helena are saving for a holiday in the summer. Well, Ethan is. I think she's too lazy to get a job.'

'What does he see in her?'

'Jennifer! You're as bad as Malcolm.'

Jennifer took a sip of ginger tea.

'Oh, you're both right. Malcolm isn't at all a fan of hers. She's not great, to be honest. I meant to tell you. Remember the teddy? The size ten teddy that Ethan bought for Helena?'

'Ye...es. I think so. The one you got in a tizz about?'

'Yes, but never mind that. It turns out, it wasn't for Helena.'

'How do you know?'

'It came up in conversation last week. I happened to mention it in passing and she knew nothing about it. Well, I mentioned the flowers. She knew nothing about them.'

Jennifer took another sip of ginger tea. The mug was large and she held it to her face for as long as she could get away with. 'I see,' she said in the end, putting the mug down. 'Do you fancy a biscuit?'

'What do you have?'

'Digestives or ginger snaps.'

'Ginger snaps, please.'

'Good choice, lady.'

As they crunched their biscuits, Jennifer said, 'Has Ethan got a bit on the side, then?'

'Jennifer!'

'You know what I mean.'

'It looks that way.'

'Can't blame him, really, can you?'

'Are you and Malcolm twins?!'

'He's eighteen, Ally. He's a young man, and he needs his fun.'

'There's fun, and there's *fun*.'

'And what does that mean, may I ask?'

'I didn't bring him up to be a womaniser.'

Jennifer almost spat out her ginger tea. '*Womaniser*?'

'It's not funny, Jennifer.'

'It is, a bit. Come off it. He's eighteen.'

'I was engaged to Malcolm at that age.'

'Yes. Well.'

'I know you don't approve of monogamy, but I do.'

'I admit it. I don't approve. I'm a fully-fledged *maniser*.'

'I know that.'

They smiled at each other. The contrast between them a thing of wonder to both of them. The friendship surviving against all the odds. Opposites attracted, Alison supposed. And they really were opposites.

They finished their tea and Alison asked if she could do anything useful. Empty the dishwasher? Hang out some laundry? Mop the floors?

'Kimberley cleaned yesterday. I'm all up to date.'

'She sounds efficient.'

'Yes. She is. Brilliant cleaner. Highly recommended if you ever need one.'

'I don't.' Alison looked around the kitchen. She noticed a large pile of clothes in the utility "corner". 'Shall I put those away for you?' she asked, pointing at the pile.

'Would you mind? I already get puffed just walking up the stairs slowly. Is that normal?'

'It's normal. Pregnancy is extremely tiring, as I recall. I'll put that pile away for you. Go and put your feet up.'

Jennifer's bedroom was large, dominated by the king size bed and two voluminous double wardrobes. She had a lot of clothes, of course. Alison opened one of the wardrobe doors and wondered how much of all her gear Jennifer could no longer fit into. She had this thought with a smattering of satisfaction. She wasn't exactly jealous of Jennifer; never had been. But to think of her pregnant, gaining weight, shutting clothes away out of sight and out of mind, temporarily, of course, was secretly rather satisfying. Alison had no doubt that Jennifer would work hard to get her slim figure back within a few weeks of the birth. She had a home gym, of course. She used it most days. Perhaps not now, not so much... she would have to ask her...

What an awful mess both wardrobes were in. This was unlike Jennifer, but that was pregnancy for you. The tiredness could be overwhelming. Perhaps she didn't allow Kimberley to help with clothes. *I'll have a quick spruce up*, thought Alison, and she set to.

She pulled out a couple of dresses, shook them and hung them up. A beautiful yellow cardigan, a fitted shape. A couple of pairs of finely tailored trousers, a bit crumpled, but they would probably uncrease if hung. What else? She pulled out a bundle of underwear. Nighties, negligees. There must be a drawer for those. She went to the chest of drawers that stood between the wardrobes. The third draw down seemed to be the right one for this sort of thing. She started to rearrange it. Then she stopped. She stared. She blinked. She pulled out a champagne-coloured garment. She checked the label. Her breathing was coming quick and shallow. She felt... what? Fear? Was it *fear*? Size ten.

Nausea. She felt nausea.

Hurriedly, dismayed, confused, fighting tears, she flung the teddy on to the bed. Then she had to sit down, and plonked herself on the bed. Then she leaped off it, images crowding in. Images she did not want to see.

The *bit on the side*. The yellow flowers. Oh god. OH GOD!

Then: a new thought. The worst of all. She had to sit down again. She burst into tears.

This couldn't be happening! She checked the label on the teddy again. It was the one. It had to be. But she'd got things wrong before, hadn't she? Got the wrong end of the stick? Flown off the handle for no good reason? She wiped her tears. She wished Malcolm was there.

'You all right?' called Jennifer.

Alison stuffed the teddy into her jeans pocket. Evidence. She was keeping it. 'Just about done!' she called back, trying to keep any wobbles out of her voice.

Wait. No. What the hell was she thinking? This friend was no *friend*! She was a... *bitch*, no more, no less, and she always had been. Why had she *ever* believed in her? In their "friendship"? There was no friendship. Friends didn't— there was no friendship. It was simple, and now perfectly clear. Nothing had ever been clearer to Alison than this feeling, at this moment. Betrayal. She stood. She checked her tear-stained face in the mirror. She decided it didn't matter. She took the silk champagne teddy, size ten, from her pocket. She looped the spaghetti straps over her index finger. She went out on to the expansive landing, its rich soft cream-coloured carpet cushioning her feet. She descended the staircase, one step at a time.

Showdown

Jennifer looked up as Alison appeared, ghost-like, in the kitchen doorway. She was as pale as a ghost at least; and in a rush of panic, Jennifer saw why. The silk champagne teddy swinging from Alison's trembling hand. Oh no... she'd forgotten that. Didn't even think of—

'You want to tell me what's been going on?' said Alison, but not Alison. This new version of Alison advanced towards her.

Jennifer sat up straight. 'Ally—'

'This is *the* teddy, isn't it?' said Alison, almost spitting the words. Jennifer had never seen her so angry. 'The one Ethan "bought for Helena". Back in November. The one I discovered the day before your birthday.'

'My memory is a bit hazy, but it certainly looked like that.'

'Yes, it did, didn't it? This one has the supermarket label. And it's a size ten. And it's what I call a champagne colour.'

What could Jennifer say? Where could she go from there? She could lie her way out of it. But somehow, it didn't feel right. Alison might appear to be, at times, but she was not, a fool. Perhaps it might be better to brazen this one out. Take Alison's wrath as her penance. Or something like that.

'Alison, I can exp—'

'Don't say that!'

'All right.'

Jake wandered through from the kitchen. He pushed past Alison and made his way to Jennifer. He put his head on her lap. 'It's all right, Jakey,' said Jennifer, stroking his head. 'Want a turn in the garden?'

Jake's ears pricked up, and Jennifer rose from the sofa, opened the French window into the rear garden, and let him out. He bumbled off, sniffing at plants as he went.

'He doesn't like arguing,' said Jennifer, and she remembered the bite he'd taken out of Patrick's hand. The blood. 'He's getting on, but he still could... get upset.'

'Is that a threat?'

'Don't be so ridiculous! I've let him out precisely so he doesn't get upset.'

'Have you had sex with my son? *My* Ethan?'

What to say? This increasingly didn't feel like a lying situation. She, finally, had been well and truly caught out. Damn that teddy! This pregnancy! Her muddled thinking. Her lack of thinking. Jennifer went to the kitchen island. She fiddled with the mugs sitting there. She was glad to have the island between her and Alison.

'Yes. Alison. I did. Not now, it's over, but yes, I did.'

Alison's face seemed to make its way through a dozen different emotions. 'And is my son the father of this... child?' Alison managed at last, pointing at Jennifer's small bump. The silk teddy still swung from her finger.

Moment of truth. What would be simpler? Deny it? Admit it? End the friendship for ever? That had happened anyway, Jennifer guessed. She had never seen Alison so cold, so upset. But denial was still the best bet. On no account did she want Ethan, Alison, Malcolm, the entire Timmins clan, knowing that this baby was Ethan's. It must never come out.

'Of course not.'

'Why "Of course" not?'

'Alison. I know who the father is, and it's not Ethan.'

'Who then?'

Think. *Think.*

'You wouldn't know who if I told you. So it's not important. Like I said, I'm going it alone.'

'More alone than you imagined!'

Jennifer bit her lip. The tears were coming, she knew, from both of them. Jennifer hated to cry.

'Is it Scott, the hunky gardener's? What would the lovely Kimberley have to say about that, I wonder?'

'It's not Scott, no. I've already told you that. I've not had sex with Scott, but I don't suppose you believe me. You seem to think I have sex with any man that crosses my path.'

'You do!'

'No, Alison, I don't.'

'But you had sex with my Ethan. By your own admission.'

'I'm just trying to be honest.'

'You're never honest. You're the most insincere and duplicitous person I think I've ever known.'

'Charming.'

'*I'm* just trying to be honest.'

Silence descended, long and painful. Neither woman knew where to look, so they both studied Jake as he continued his sniffing around in the garden.

'I once thought we were friends,' said Alison. 'But now I finally know better. Bigger fool me. Dozy Alison, married to dozy Malcolm, with one dozy child. Just one child who I love more than anyone in this world and you had to go and...*sully* him. What on earth were you thinking?'

'Ethan is eighteen.'

'You're his aunt! It's obscene! Abusive!'

'Now, hang on—'

'No. You hang on. You're his Aunty Jennifer.'

'I'm not his aunt, Alison. I'm not.'

'You're the closest thing he has to one.' And that was that, Alison's face crumpled and the tears came.

'I know. I'm sorry.'

'So w-why'd you d-do it? Such a horrible thing?'

'A moment of weakness. That's all I can say.'

'Was it j-j-just one moment of weakness, or several?'

'Sit down, Alison, please.'

'I'm fine here.'

'Ethan and I... saw each other... a few times. Then I decided it was all wrong and... misguided. So I ended it.'

'I see. "Misguided"?'

'I apologise.'

'For what? Breaking my heart?'

'Yes, if you like.'

Alison wiped her eyes, her nose, with the teddy. She didn't seem to notice. Jennifer made a mental note to put the teddy in the bin – where it belonged.

'I'm going now,' said Alison, making a huge shuddering effort to stop crying. 'Our friendship is officially over. I want you to know that. Don't come near me or my family ever again.'

'Aliso—'

'No. I mean it this time. It's over. All those years... There's no *trust* anymore. Goodbye, Jennifer. Good luck with your baby. The poor little sod.'

And she dropped the snot-and-tears-ridden teddy on to the floor; she turned away from Jennifer, and left.

The Phone Call

When her phone rang early the following morning, Alison wasn't entirely surprised. She really should change the ringtone. It was so... demanding. She'd get Ethan to change it for her.

Jennifer was calling. A well-timed call, eleven minutes past eight; knowing that Malcolm had just left for work and Ethan for college. Alison let it ring. She'd pick up on the second call.

Which didn't materialise. It wasn't like Jennifer to not try again. But things were different now. They would never be the same again.

Sometimes, and especially now, at this time, Alison wished she had never met Jennifer. That first day at the new school, Jennifer plucking her out of the throng, becoming her protector, really. Alison had been grateful at the time... she had been grateful for many years. But not now. Look what it had led to. A betrayal of the worst kind. Jennifer was a false friend. She could see that now. Selfish, vain, exploitative.

Last night over dinner she could barely bring herself to look at her son, who chomped on his lasagne, chips, and green beans, with his usual gusto and abandon. She had said nothing at all to Malcolm. She didn't know what to say. Half the night she had lain awake, fretting, listening to Malcolm's soft breathing. He had never, thank goodness, been a snorer. The situation had reeled round and round in her mind until in the end she'd got up at half past five and made coffee.

Now, she showered, dressed, put a load of laundry on, made another coffee. She checked her phone. Jennifer still hadn't called back. She called Jennifer.

'Jennifer Sawyer.'

'It's me.'

'I know. I was just testing.'

'Testing what, pray?'

'I'm not sure. Forget I said that. Are you all right, Ally?'

'What do you think?'

'I am sorry. It was such a stupid mistake.'

'It's much worse than that.'

'Yes. I know. But it is over, Alison.'

'It can't ever be "over", Jennifer. It's done, it's out there, I know it happened.'

'What do you want me to say?'

'Admit that you're a slut. A damaging, selfish, slut.'

'Alison!'

'That's what you are.'

'Maybe so, but you're my friend.'

'No. I'm not. I *was*. Actually... no, I never was. I was just your pet. A dumpy little accessory. Somebody to make you look good when you needed to use her.'

'That's not fair and it's certainly not true.'

'What do you know about being fair and true?'

The pause was long, fretful. Alison wondered if Jennifer was even still there.

Then: 'All right, Little Miss Holier-Than-Thou. Fair and true? I take it Malcolm still doesn't know about your little... dalliance... with the lovely Danny?'

Alison felt herself boil up red. Her throat constricted. 'Don't you dare... that was years ago!'

'So what? You aren't really in any position to judge me.'

'Yes I am. Danny was my age and he wasn't my best friend's son! I can certainly judge a predatory woman like you.'

Silence again. Alison fought tears.

'Alison?' Jennifer's voice was cold, hard.

'What?'

'You've insulted me once too often. How dare you call me predatory? Can't you hear how awful that is? An awful thing for one woman to say to another?'

'I—'

'So I quite agree, we are no longer friends. So I may as well tell you the truth. It's only fair, after all, isn't it?'

'You've already told me the truth!'

'No. I haven't.'

'What do you mean?' *Perhaps she didn't actually have sex with Ethan? Please, please...*

'Ethan is the father of my baby. I'm carrying your grandchild. Stick that in your holy little truth pipe and smoke it. Now, goodbye, Alison. Until you come to your senses, goodbye.'

Alison screamed. She threw her phone across the room. Luckily, it didn't break.

After the Phone Call

Jennifer stroked Jake and felt herself tremble, which wasn't like her. Must be the pregnancy, playing with her emotions. Causing havoc with her emotions. She shouldn't have told Alison. Now she really had gone and done it. Now it really was "out there".

Oh God! What if she told Ethan? Of course she would tell Ethan. But that wouldn't be right. He should hear it from her first, shouldn't he? Had she been a coward? Had she made the wrong decision? She could have just had this "seen to" weeks ago, with Rose, at the clinic. Nobody would ever have known. That might have been the simpler thing to do, the easiest.

But life wasn't easy, was it? Was it ever meant to be?

She'd lost a friend. No. Who was she kidding? She'd lost her *only* friend. *The* friend. Dear, sweet, annoying, prickly, naïve, kind, Alison. Ally Pally.

Daughter, husband, friend. All gone. The husband, great, he'd needed to go. The daughter? Well, Jennifer's decision at the time. Any pain she felt had long ago been pushed down deep inside. Perhaps it was that which drove her pursuit of men? Alison was right. She was predatory, wasn't she? Using men for sex. Gratification. Fun. Then dropping them, like hot rocks. At least one of those men had been deeply hurt. He had been in love with her, she supposed. But she had shut him out, blocked him, refused to listen to his tears and lamentations. They were nothing compared to hers.

She was a mess. Calm exterior, seething interior. Sex was her drug, her emotional crutch. Knowing that men wanted to sleep with her gave her such a feeling of... power, she supposed. No. Not power. Control. That was the word. But now her life, so long "controlled", was no longer under control. It was unravelling, and it was alarming.

She hugged Jake. He accepted her hug in the simple accepting way he had, with grace.

Thank God for dogs.

But she would have to ring Ethan. She must try to speak to him before Alison did.

The doorbell rang at lunchtime. Jake, barking, loped along the hallway. Jennifer followed. Holding Jake's collar, she opened the door. Jake's warnings turned to delight when he realised it was Ethan. He'd always liked Ethan. Jake took his fussings, and then led Jennifer back towards the kitchen, tail wagging.

'Come on through,' said Jennifer, as she followed Jake. Ethan obediently followed her. In the kitchen, Jennifer stood behind her kitchen island, Jake at her side. Ethan hovered in the kitchen doorway. 'Thanks for coming, Ethan.'

'Are you... all right?' he said.

'No. Not really. Look, I may as well just tell you straight. You are the father of this baby. I was never going to let on, but I had a row with your mother and it all came out. And I'm sorry about that. I think she's vowed never to speak to me again. I thought you should hear the news from me.'

Ethan turned pale. He made for the kitchen island, and leaned on it, head in hands. Rather dramatically, Jennifer thought.

'Ethan?

He looked up, then stood up, straight and tall. 'Are you sure?'

'Yes. I'm sure. I must admit at first I assumed it was another man's. I was sure of it to begin with. But the scans and dates prove otherwise.'

'Oh. Right.'

'Is that all you have to say?'

'And Mum knows?'

'Yes, afraid so. That was my fault. We got into a row. She was unkind and I lashed out and the truth tumbled out. Like it tends to do, you know?'

'I can't believe this. Are you *sure*?'

'Yes! Ethan! I'm bloody sure. OK?'

'And you've fallen out with Mum.'

'Yes. She thinks I'm some kind of pervert.'

'Right. I'll have to talk to her then. She doesn't need to be so silly.'

'Silly?'

'You know what I mean. She overreacts.'

'Less about your mum. She'll get over it. I want to talk about the baby.'

'OK.'

'I've made a decision, which is I'm going it alone. You're too young to be a proper father. In time, as you grow older, you can help out financially. But that's in the future. You need to grow and mature and get a career going before you can be a father. So there are no expectations. You can see the baby whenever you like, but financial stuff can come later.'

'Will you name me on the birth certificate?'

'No. I don't think so.'

'Oh. Is that good or bad?'

'Neither. It's just the right thing to do. Plus I don't want my child to be saddled with Timmins for a surname.'

'Oh. Right. But—'

'Ethan, it's a lot for you to take in, I know that. I will never be a bitch and stop you spending time with this child. It's yours as much as it's mine. But right now you are a kid yourself and I'm not. I can handle this, and it's not as if I'm short of a bob or two.'

'A what or two?'

'I can afford to raise this child.'

'Right. Yeah. Of course.'

'You can't. Not yet. One day, yes. And that's quite apart from the emotional stuff.'

'What do you mean?'

'Maturity. Emotional intelligence.'

'I'm not a complete twat, Aunty Jennifer.'

'I know that. But you are a... new adult. Young, and carefree, and I want you to know it's fine by me if you stay that way for as long as you should. I'm not going to make any financial or emotional demands. In ten years time, perhaps, yes, by then you can be helping out. I hope you'll want to. But...' Jennifer, for the first time, felt wobbly, 'if you decide you can't, or don't want to, acknowledge this child, that's fine too. I mean, it will do. It's OK. I will accept that.'

Ethan seemed to be in deep thought. She wasn't sure if he ever thought much about anything. He was still pale. He looked young and scared and shocked. Only natural, she supposed. Jennifer sat down on one of her kitchen island stools. 'Would you like a cup of tea?' she offered. 'A glass of water?'

'No thanks. I need to get back to college. Can I... think? Can I have time to think about all this, I mean?'

'All the time in the world.'

'I'm sorry, Aunty Jennifer. I really am. I never thought...'

'No. Me neither. But it's happened. Go talk to your folks.'

'That's going to be a difficult chat.'

'We all have those in life, young Ethan.'

'I have to go.'

'OK.'

Jennifer and Jake followed Ethan to the front door. He opened it, stepped out. Scott the hunky gardener was cutting the grass. He waved.

'See yer, Aunty Jennifer.'

'See you, Ethan. And don't you think it's time we dropped "aunty"?'

'Yes. Probably.'

'Great. No more Aunty Jennifer.'

No More Aunty Jennifer

On autopilot, Alison prepared the evening meal: cauliflower cheese with mashed potato. *Creamed* potato. She planned to add lots of cheese to the sauce, far more than any recipe ever advised. You could never have too much cheese. It was impossible.

Just like Ethan being a father was impossible. How was she going to tell Malcolm? Should she simply raise it over dinner? Speak to Ethan first? Say nothing and wait for him to tell her? She wasn't sure if she could even talk about it at all. Too painful, too difficult, too incomprehensible. The shame! Was that even the right word? Embarrassment, perhaps?

She opened a bottle of Pinot Grigio and poured herself a large glass. She grated the cheese for the sauce. She took a clump of the grated cheese and stuffed it into her mouth. Always a difficult snack. Half the cheese landed on the floor. She picked it up, looked at it. She popped it into the pan with the rest of the cheese, and stirred the sauce vigorously. She didn't want any lumps.

'Mum? Dad? I have to talk to you. Mum... you know what about, don't you?'

Alison took a swig of wine. She was on her third glass. She had opened another bottle so Malcolm could have some with his dinner. She had not thought Ethan would just raise the matter like this.

'What's all this, then?' said Malcolm cheerfully.

Alison cleared her throat. 'Malcolm. I'm afr—'

'Mum, no. Stop. Let me tell Dad, please. Please.'

Alison slumped back in her chair. She fiddled with the stem of her wine glass.

Malcolm looked from her to Ethan. 'Somebody say something,' said Malcolm.

Ethan took a swig of his wine, then wiped his mouth with his sleeve. He put the wine down. 'I'm going to be a father.'

Malcolm was still and silent. *Say something, Malcolm!*

'But you're both so young,' said Malcolm. His voice wobbled. Was he on the verge of tears?

Alison cleared her throat again, and glared at Ethan, who turned bright red.

'Mum,' said Ethan, 'I know it's difficult for you...'

'No shit!'

Malcolm and Ethan stared at her, shocked. She never swore. She *rarely* swore.

'Steady on, Alison,' said Malcolm. 'They are both adults, at the end of the day.'

'Ethan,' said Alison, 'please put your father in the picture.'

Ethan took another swig of wine. All three plates of cauliflower cheese were cooling and congealing. So much for her efforts.

'What's going on?' said Malcolm.

'Dad... It isn't Helena.'

Malcolm looked, once again, like a guppy fish. 'Not Helena?' he said in the end.

'Oh, Malcolm...'

'Then who is it? Who's pregnant?'

Alison and Ethan looked at each other. Malcolm waited.

Alison took another gulp of wine while she waited. Then Malcolm grew pale.

'That's right. It's Jennifer!' shouted Alison. 'His *Aunty* Jennifer!'

'She's not my aun—'

'*Jennifer?!*'

'Dad... it was a fling, you see? A stupid thing.'

'*Jennifer?*'

'Yes, Malcolm, Jennifer. Jennifer is the mother of our grandchild!' Alison burst into tears.

'You and *Jennifer?*'

'Dad, can we move beyond that bit now, please? Mum, don't cry. It's going to be all right. I saw Jennifer today and—'

'T-t-today?'

'Yes, Mum, today. She asked me to go and see her at lunch time and she told me about your row... and... she was really nice and sensible. She doesn't expect me to pay for anything until I'm older.'

'*Pay* for anything?'

'Yes. You know, baby stuff costs money? Kids cost money?'

'Yes, I'm well aware of that Ethan, thank you!'

'And she said I can be as involved, or not, as I want to be.'

Alison shook her head, drank more wine. Pushed her plate away. 'How generous of her.'

'I agree,' said Malcolm, and he smiled at his son, kindly as ever. 'It is generous of her.'

'Oh for god's sake!' cried Alison.

'It'll be all right, Mum, Dad,' said Ethan. 'I know it's a shock. But it's my shock more than it's yours.'

'It's a bloody mess!'

'Alison...' said Malcolm.

'Well, it is! He's too young to be a father, she's too old to be a mother! And quite apart from anything else, she's a pervert!'

'Alison, for goodness sake...'

'Mum. I'm an adult. It was stupid, of course, but she's not a pervert.'

'What the hell is she then?'

'She's lonely,' said Malcolm, and the room fell silent.

Alison stood and picked up her plate. 'I'm microwaving this. I refuse to waste good food.'

'Good idea, my love,' said Malcolm. 'I'll do the same. He turned to Ethan. 'Does Helena know?'

Helena

Alison bundled laundry into the tumble dryer and turned it on for fifty minutes. She didn't like to tumble dry. It was expensive and it wore clothes out too quickly. But it was wet outside, with a cold hard rain drumming relentlessly on the windows. She also didn't like clothes hanging around on airers for days on end. Perhaps if she had a separate laundry room that might work. Or a laundry "end" in the kitchen, like Jennifer had. But their kitchen was too small for such luxuries. The washing machine was crammed in under the kitchen counter alongside the fridge.

Jennifer. Alison had removed her name and number from her phone. She had torn out her page from her address book. She had gone through her wardrobe, taking out all the clothes Jennifer had ever bought for her. These she had laid out on the bed. With regret, she had folded up the garments, one by one, and placed them in a couple of carrier bags, to take them to the charity shop. Not the one she used to volunteer in. She would take these clothes to a different one.

How on earth could Jennifer have been so... revolting? Utterly revolting. Malcolm almost defending her! He certainly had not been angry, not really. Not that Malcolm ever did become angry. It wasn't in his emotional repertoire. Tearful, yes, upset, yes; confused, yes. But he didn't feel any of these things, it seemed, about Ethan having a child with Jennifer. Apparently that was "OK". If not OK, acceptable... he was *perturbed*, he said. Any father would be. Perturbed for his son. Perturbed?! Pathetic. He should be furious, storm around to Jennifer's mansion and have it out with her.

And Ethan, too, not as uptight as she'd assumed he would be. Not as embarrassed either. Yet the situation was wholly embarrassing, particularly for Jennifer, who also hadn't seemed embarrassed. Or perturbed. This really was it for their friendship. The end. The *very* end. No going back, no recovery, no reconciliation. Ever. Never. Malcolm could accuse her of overreacting all he liked. She wasn't overreacting. She was reacting appropriately, which was better than underreacting, which, it seemed, was how everybody else was feeling. Underwhelmed. Cool with it. If not cool, calm. What was there to be calm about?

Her mobile rang. A number she didn't recognise. Not Jennifer's, which she knew by heart. She answered the call.

'Alison?'

'Yes.'

'It's Helena.'

She was crying. Ethan must have—

'Ethan told me what's h-h-happened.'

'I see.'

'It's devastating. I thought... I thought we were in love. Together.'

'I know. I thought so too. Would you like to come round for a coffee?'

Alison hastily made a batch of chocolate biscuits. The melt-in-your-mouth ones that were her speciality. The doorbell rang just as she was taking them from the oven. Perfect timing. Not that life would ever be perfect again.

Helena was red-faced and sniffing. She shuffled through to the lounge and threw herself dramatically on to the sofa. She hadn't removed her trainers, and had tracked in wet mud. Alison resolved to ignore it. She would allow it to dry and clean it up later. The poor girl was beside herself. As others should be.

'I have finished with Ethan,' Helena said, sniffing loudly.

'Have a biscuit,' said Alison, offering the plate.

Helena took one, and took a bite. 'I can't believe he could do such a thing.'

'I know. I can't believe it either. Awful.'

'To cheat on me with—'

'His aunt!'

'She's not his aunt, Alison.'

'She's the closest he'll ever have to one.'

'She's a tart.'

'Yes.'

'He's a bastard!'

'Well, almost. I'll go and get you a coffee. Have another biscuit.'

'Tea please. I'm not in the mood for coffee.' She started to cry again.

Really, Helena! Ethan was not a bastard. He was a *victim*. But poor Helena was upset. It was understandable.

Alison made drinks for them both. On her arrival back in the lounge Helena had ceased her crying and the plate of biscuits was half-empty. 'Here you are,' said Alison, handing Helena a mug.

Alison took a biscuit, looked at it for a few moments, then put it back on the plate. She had no appetite.

'I hate him,' said Helena, quiet, a look of resolve about her that Alison had not seen before.

'I know. I hate her.'

'Me too. How could she?'

'She has a track record. It's what she does.'

'Sleeping with people much younger than her?'

'She sleeps with a lot of men. That's what I meant. Some of them are bound to be younger than her.'

'Ethan should have known better!'

'Yes, he should. So should she.'

'It's revolting.'

'Yes. Have another biscuit. I can always make some more later for Malcolm and Ethan.'

'I-I-I'm going to miss you... all. Coming round h-h-here has always been really nice.'

'Oh, Helena, love. You can come and see me. There is no need for us to fall out. If you need to talk, you pop round.'

'It's going to be so awkward at college.'

'You don't have that much longer left though, do you? Exams in May and June?'

'Yeah.'

'Then it will all be over and you can go your separate ways for ever.'

Helena sniffed. She took another biscuit. Only three of the original twelve remained on the plate. *Goodness me, this girl can eat.* But she was stressed, hurt, upset. And fresh, warm, home-baked chocolate biscuits were always a great comfort. Alison might have done the same herself. She found her thoughts bending towards the tin of Quality Street she had secreted away before Christmas in the back of her wardrobe. It was either those, or the even more secret packet of cigarettes and the disposable lighter that she kept at the back of her bottom drawer, hidden behind silk scarves, chiffon scarves, polyester scarves, fluffy bed socks that were somehow not comfortable, boxes of old jewellery, and bath sets not yet used. Nobody knew about her cigarettes, not even Jennifer. Now she never would know. Alison stifled her thoughts, pressed upon Helena yet another biscuit, and felt a wave of relief wash over her when the girl finally left.

Alison retrieved the trappings of her hidden vice and went out into the rain-soaked back garden. She lit a cigarette, blew a smoke ring (her only trick) and although she wanted to cry, she found she couldn't.

SPRING

Test Results

Jennifer stood straight, or at least as straight as she could (she was having back pains) and studied her bump in the gilt bathroom mirror. God, she was ENORMOUS! And still another twelve weeks to go... possibly more if the baby decided to hang on in there.

Her outfits nowadays consisted of men's shirts, size 16 leggings and T-shirts, trainers, and huge, cotton, comfortable underwear. Her bras were measuring 38D, a size she had never dreamt of. She had been a 32B since the age of fourteen. She was fat. Her legs were fat, her arms were fat, her face puffy... yet her skin was all right, she had to admit. The skin on her face, at least. It was fresh-looking, a nice colour, and just as well because she couldn't be bothered with much make-up these days. The skin on her belly was not going to come out of this intact. Stretch marks had started weeks ago. She had avoided them in her first pregnancy. Perhaps being that much younger had literally saved her skin.

Her baby girl kicked. Jennifer put her hand down to her belly.

'Hello, you.'

Her girl kicked again. She was going to be bright. But Jennifer suspected all mums-to-be thought their baby would be bright.

Jennifer had eschewed ante-natal classes, where she would only be a granny figure, vaguely embarrassing to the younger women; and she had nobody to go with. Confident she might be, but pregnancy demanded a whole new level of courage. Her midwife tried to persuade her to go to the classes. Jennifer politely declined. Instead she bought a couple of "good" baby books, and read them with mild interest. At the check-ups, the midwife listened for the baby's heartbeat, tested Jennifer's urine, and had arranged the amniocentesis at the end of February. That had hurt, that needle. But the result was negative. Nothing wrong detected. It wasn't entirely accurate, and the baby could still have chromosomal abnormalities. She was offered further tests, which she declined. No more needles. For now, at least. What would be, would be. Her baby girl would be who she was, tests or no tests. No going back now.

She did want to know the sex of her baby, and had been delighted, beyond delighted, to discover at twenty weeks that she was going to have a girl. But she hadn't told anybody else. Her secret. And who was there to tell, truly?

The amnio results had arrived a week or so after the test; Jennifer had cried, a bit (she cried often, sometimes at nothing at all), and her first thought had been she must let Alison know. Then it hit her. Again.

She had not heard from Alison since the phone call the day after she had stormed from her house, angry, tearful, on Teddy Gate day. Way back in February. It felt like years ago, not a couple of months. She had tried ringing, but she couldn't get through. Alison had probably blocked her number. She had e-mailed; again, no reply. She had even popped round in her Honda LS one Monday morning (Alison was always in on Mondays, her laundry day) but nobody came to the door. Jennifer had the feeling that Alison had peeped out of her bedroom window, seen the car, and refused to respond. Alison-like behaviour. She was too stubborn for her own good.

Jennifer had rang Ethan to let him know the result. He had been happy, she thought. "OK with it" like the youngsters were these days. He must have told Malcolm because he texted her a day or two later, saying what good news it was and was there anything she needed, and could he help? Bless him. What a man. Jennifer had never felt so generously disposed towards Malcolm. She hoped Alison knew what she had in her husband. Boring, yes. Kind, yes. With bells on. And that was all that mattered, when you came down to it. Jennifer needed all the kindness she could get.

She had a shower, dried, put on her comfy undies, her massive bra, a baggy T, and those voluminous black leggings. As she slowly made her way downstairs, sideways, her doorbell rang. Would it be Alison this time? She hoped it would be, every time. But it was only ever the postman, or an Amazon delivery, or Scott, needing to ask her something about the garden. She wondered which of the three it would be this time. She hadn't ordered anything recently. Scott wasn't there today. He had three long term clients and spread his working week (Monday to Saturday) evenly around all three. Jennifer's days were Mondays and Thursdays.

It must be the postman, but what was he bringing? She opened the door. A young woman stood before her. She clutched a large red bag in front of her body. She was pretty. Dark-haired. Brown-eyed. Black-clothed. Red-lipsticked. *Very* pretty. And all this filed neatly and briskly through Jennifer's mind even as the young woman said 'Mum?'

Marnie

Jennifer stared at her daughter. It was her. She could tell from the eyes. They were her eyes. And she had her father's nose, his forehead. Noble-looking. Nice shape. He'd been a looker, her dad, if nothing else.

'Marnie?'

'Yes. Can I come in?'

Jennifer stood back, and held the door open. Marnie entered, looking around her. Jennifer closed the door and they stood in the hallway, neither of them knowing what to say or how to feel.

'How did you—?'

'I hope you—'

'Sorry,' said Jennifer. 'Go on.'

'I hope you don't mind me turning up,' said Marnie.

It was Marnie. It really was Marnie. Jennifer felt a little weak, perhaps faint. She needed to sit down. She put her hand to the wall.

'How did you find me?'

Marnie shrugged. 'The Internet. Electoral roll. It was easy.'

'I see.' *Did she though?* 'Come through to the kitchen. My dog's out in the garden.'

'What kind of dog?'

'A German shepherd. He's called Jake and he's a big softie.'

They went into the kitchen. Marnie approached the large French windows. Jake came bounding up to them, barking. Marnie took a step back.

'He'll calm down in a minute. I'll let him in when he does.'

'OK.'

'Would you like tea? Coffee?'

'Do you have ginger tea?'

'I do.'

'Are you pregnant?' Marnie stared at Jennifer's bump.

'I am. Twenty-eight weeks.'

Marnie laughed. 'Oh my god!'

'I know. I'm a very old mother, I'm afraid.'

'It's not that!'

Marnie put down her big red bag to reveal a substantial bump of her own.

'Oh!' said Jennifer.

'Shall we make that two ginger teas?'

Marnie was twenty-five weeks pregnant. An "accidental" pregnancy, just like Jennifer's. The father a fly-by-night, from what Jennifer could gather. Jennifer didn't mention her baby's father, or Malcolm, or Alison.

'But I've no money. I've fallen out with my mum. I haven't spoken to her since I was eighteen.'

'Why not?'

Marnie shrugged again. 'So I was renting a place with another girl but she moved out and... well... I'm skint and have nowhere to go. I lost my job.'

Jennifer was increasingly uneasy. 'I see. What about your father?'

'I don't have one. Not anymore.'

'I'm sorry.'

'Are you?'

'Yes.'

'I thought I could stay here. Just until I'm on my feet again.'

'Here?'

'Yes. You are my actual mum.'

'In one way. I'm your mother. But I'm not your mum.'

'You could be my mum now though.'

Jake stood at the French windows, softly panting, waiting patiently. 'Would you be OK if I let him in?' said Jennifer.

'Sure.'

Marnie looked nervous but Jake would be an ice-breaker and bring to an end the uncomfortable conversation. The awkward request. Stay here? No! No way. That was not going to happen.

Jake bounded in and had a thorough sniff of Marnie's shoes, legs. She tentatively patted his head.

'Good boy, Jake,' said Jennifer, and handed Marnie a dog biscuit to give him. He took it and sloped off with it to his bed by the windows. 'He likes you, I think,' said Jennifer.

'Perhaps he can tell we're related.'

'Perhaps.'

'We might smell the same. Give off the same chemicals.'

'Interesting thought.'

'Could I say here?'

Jennifer picked up their empty mugs and took them to the sink. Marnie sat at the island, half an eye on Jake, half an eye on Jennifer. Jennifer turned to face Marnie. 'I'm not sure it's a good idea.'

'Why?'

'We barely know each other. We've only just met, for heaven's sake.'

'And whose fault is that?'

'Mine. I know it's mine. I gave you up. My decision. I wasn't pressured. I was twenty-five.'

'Why did you give me up?'

'I never wanted a child. You were a shock. I also didn't want another termination.'

'Oh. I see.'

'I had an abortion when I was fifteen. I thought I might never be able to have kids then I realised I was pregnant with you and—'

'And you decided to dump me into the care system.'

'Yes. I suppose so. I gave you up for adoption.'

'I never was adopted. You know that, right?'

'I didn't know. What happened?'

'I was fostered. Long term, in the end.'

'And that was as good as adoption? Wasn't it?'

'I went though half a dozen foster homes before settling with my mum and dad. It was a long-term foster placement, finally. At the age of twelve.'

'I'm sorry to hear that.'

'I was shoved from pillar to post for twelve years just when I needed security.'

'I am sorry. Truly.'

'You know it didn't have to be a clean break situation? We could have kept in touch.'

'I know. I thought it best not to.'

'Best for who?'

Jennifer went to Jake, taking up his bowl to replenish the water. 'For you, I think. I wasn't mother material. I didn't deserve you.'

'But what about me? I deserved you.' Marnie took another big look around. 'You can't tell me you didn't have the space.'

'At that time I was in a very small flat, with one bedroom. This came later.'

'Whatever.'

'I had no space in my heart, I suppose. No real role models.'

'So? Neither have I! A foster mum who only half-loved me. She preferred her natural daughter. Of course she did! A foster dad I didn't really ever get to know who ran off with another woman. It wasn't a terrible home, but it wasn't that great either.'

'I'm sorry. You deserved more.'

'I deserved my real mum.'

Jennifer put Jake's bowl back down on his mat next to his bed. He stood and slurped the water. Jennifer stroked his back.

'That dog means more to you than I do. Where did you get him?'

'My ex-husband and I bought him as a puppy.'

'Not a rescue dog then?'

'No.'

'What happened to your marriage?'

'It didn't work out.'

'Why?' This seemed to be Marnie's favourite question. 'Was he my dad?

'No, no. Your dad was... a boyfriend. Nobody special. I never even told him I was pregnant, and we broke up. Have you tracked him down too?'

'Not yet.'

'You don't need to! He was a waste of space.'

'That's nice.'

'Sorry, but he was. All the men I've ever been in relationships with were. I'm a romantic disaster. No good in relationships.'

'And?'

'And... that's it. I'm not very good at relationships, at all. Any of them. Friendships, even.'

'Are you giving this baby up too?'

Jennifer returned to the kettle, filled it, flicked it on again.

'More ginger tea?'

'Yes please.'

'I'm keeping this baby.'

Marnie nodded, bit her bottom lip. Her eyes filled with tears, which, in a valiant effort, she managed to hold in. Jake, restless, wandered over to her. Marnie put down her hand and he licked it. He must like her, Jennifer thought. He didn't lick everybody's hands.

'I'm keeping my baby too,' Marnie said.

'I'm pleased for you.'

'I wouldn't dream of doing anything else.'

'How did you get here?' asked Jennifer. *Where did she live? Where had she travelled from? Was she tired? She looked tired.*

'Train and taxi.'

'Did you come far?'

'From London.'

'Not too far away then.'

'It sure feels that way.'

'Yes. I'm sure it does.'

'Can I stay? Please? I won't be in the way and it's not like you don't have a spare room, is it? You must have at least six bedrooms here.'

Jake wandered back to his bed by the window, circled, and settled down with a sigh.

'Five. But one of them is a box room.'

'OK. Four bedrooms plus a box room, whatever that is. I bet you have en suite bathrooms too, don't you?'

'One or two.'

'There we are then. Please. I... I have nowhere else to go.'

'Nowhere?'

'I have the flat, but I'm being kicked out. I can't afford the rent on my own, especially since I lost my job. Anyway, it's a room, really, not a flat. It's mouldy. It stinks. The other rooms have drug addicts living in them. Worse.'

'Look, I'm sorry, but we—'

'And I haven't told you the whole truth.'

'Which is...?'

'My foster mum died in January. My sister didn't even let me know until a few weeks later. She said *I* abandoned the family and didn't deserve to go to the funeral. She won't help me. She doesn't want to know.' And finally the long-held-in tears flowed.

Jake looked up from his bed, confused, upset. He'd never liked crying.

Weekend

The Timmins family had never quite mastered the art of Saturdays. Other families seemed to do them with style and panache. Perhaps a handsome dad in a white shirt and chinos would trot off to the local artisan bakery for fresh bread, fresh croissants; picking up coffee from a trendy local indie coffee shop. A slim and pretty mum would maybe lay the table, pour freshly-squeezed orange juice into fancy glasses. There would be newspapers. The two children, a pigeon pair, would get up without complaining and eat the artisan food, also without complaining. After breakfast, a day out... walking in the countryside, or indoor snowboarding, or ice skating, or maybe even a visit to a staid National Trust property. Cinema in the winter.

But not in the Timmins household. Somehow, they had never managed these idyllic Saturdays. Jennifer knew how to do Saturdays in style. They usually involved shopping, lunch, and cocktails. Alison, in recent years, her frequent companion.

Alison got up, at twelve minutes past six, creeping away from the snoozing Malcolm. As she tip-toed down the creaky stairs, Alison wondered if she lacked sophistication? Yes. She did. In all areas of her life. Jennifer... damn her! Why did she keep thinking of her?

In the small but always-clean kitchen, Alison made a mug

of coffee. Instant. Jennifer had one of those noisy barista machines in her large kitchen. It made wonderful coffee. But she wouldn't miss it. It was poison to her now. A poisoned chalice, which is what their entire "friendship" had been. Jennifer has merely bestowed her idea of friendship on Alison, who had been vulnerable at the time. And that is all it had ever been. There was no... equality... no *balance* to their friendship. Jennifer held all the cards: she was wealthier, prettier, taller, more stylish. Older, even. She had *bought* Alison.

Alison took her coffee into their cosy lounge. She pulled back the curtains and surveyed their small square garden. She and Malcolm were not keen or proficient gardeners, but they kept it neat-ish. They had a well-stocked bird table and the birds were using it now, the regular gang of starlings scrapping and squawking, flinging bird seed and suet chunks all over the grass. Alison enjoyed watching the garden birds and their daily battle with existence. Perhaps there was a... what was the word?... a metaphor playing out at the bird table.

She must bake some more biscuits this weekend. Helena had texted yesterday to say she would "pop round" again on Monday, after lunch. Dear Helena. Still hurting, and avoiding Ethan... who seemed to want to avoid her too. Alison felt she ought to be kind to the poor girl. And, actually, she wanted to be kind. Charitable. Understanding. Ethan had done a real number on her. As Jennifer had done a number on Ethan. And on her. But she mustn't think about Jennifer anymore. Their friendship was finally over. "That Woman", Helena had christened her.

Yet Alison's mind seemed to want to return to Jennifer. The things Jennifer had said on that awful day in February. Dragging up the past. That regrettable episode with... with Daniel. Danny. She tried not to think about him these days. So much so that he had become a mythological, fake, memory in her life. She never thought of him, of the night they had spent together. He was now merely an abstract figure, almost a figment of her desiccated imagination. It was as though she merely had access to somebody else's memory.

Oh Danny Boy

1995

Wedding preparations were all very well, but you had to have some fun too, said Jennifer. They *were* fun, protested Alison. You know what I mean, said Jennifer.

So Jennifer organised a hen-night-for-two, a week before the wedding. Alison didn't want her mother there; didn't want to invite her distant university friends; not her work colleagues. Yes, they were all going to the wedding. But she didn't really want a hen-do anyway; so a sedate dinner out, some wine, just her and Jennifer, was arranged. They hadn't been out together for a couple of years.

The London restaurant was swanky. They were to eat at seven; then, Jennifer suggested, a pub, even a nightclub? They were staying overnight in the Owen hotel, in Bloomsbury. Jennifer knew it to be a nice one. She had stayed there before. Alison didn't ask who, why, or when. The Cabernet Sauvignon was good, and when Jennifer ordered a second bottle, Alison hadn't protested. She knew she would have the mother of all hangovers in the morning. But perhaps it would be worth it. Soon she would be married, to her lovely Malcolm. And he was lovely. Perhaps a bit dull. Not much of a drinker. But tonight was for fun, friend, and wine. To hell with the consequences.

They found a pub after they had finished their meal (no dessert). Jennifer paid for everything; she would "brook no refusals". This was her idea, and her treat.

The pub was Saturday-night busy; noisy; smoky. The jukebox was blaring out Britpop. Jennifer somehow always managed to be noticed and served promptly at bars, and that evening was no different. The young man serving was good-looking: black hair and blue eyes. A combination that Alison had always found rather alluring. Jennifer ordered, and leaned in to hear what the barman said. A conversation ensued that Alison could not quite keep track of. But when he smiled at her, and made her rum and coke a double, and handed it to her with a wink, Alison found herself giving him her broadest smile. The dazzler, that's what Malcolm called it. He said it made her whole face come alive. Her whole being.

Later, as the pub gradually emptied, the handsome barman wandered over to their table.

'Would you ladies be having another drink?' His soft London-Irish accent, like the black hair and the blue eyes, another of Alison's secret weaknesses. He was slim, toned, and wore his jeans very well. Jennifer asked about local clubs. He knew of a good one, and was going on there himself after work. He could get them in.

And he did. Alison had rarely visited night clubs. This one was underground. It was playing rave music but there was a "quiet" area too, with a classy-looking bar, sofas, funky pictures on the walls. The toilets were exquisite, and clean. She thought she saw a current popstar at a distant table, but she wasn't sure.

Danny, the charming Irish barman, bought Alison and Jennifer another drink each. He sat with them on a plush sofa, chatting about his life, asking about the wedding. He was very nice. Personable. Flirtatious, but not salacious. He laughed a lot as Jennifer described the forensically precise wedding preparations. He said he couldn't imagine ever being married. Wasn't Alison fearful of losing her freedom? Her independence? How old was she? Twenty-five? Only a year older than him. He shook his head.

When Jennifer got up to go to the loo, whispering to Alison that she would "make herself scarce" for a while, Alison panicked. What on earth was she doing here, in this alien place, with this stranger? This wasn't her world, at all. It was fun, yes, but it wasn't *her*. She was getting drunk. Very drunk... freedom... independence... Malcolm, only, from her wedding day onwards... When Danny put his hand on her knee she didn't shove it off, and later, after another drink, when he kissed her she didn't shove that off either. Where was Jennifer?

Later, how much later Alison could never recall, she was in a black cab with Danny and Jennifer. Danny was holding her hand. Jennifer smiled at her: conspiratorially, supportively... that she did remember.

And what came after faded in and out... Jennifer laughing; the hotel room door closing (the next day she learned that Jennifer had managed to book into another room); Danny kissing her... but more than that: her kissing Danny and undoing his shirt. *That* she could recall with crystal clarity. She had banished guilt, all thoughts of Malcolm, and instead she had sex with Danny. The sex was just sex. Fine. Nothing wrong with Danny, as far as she could make out... it was how it made her feel that she could remember now, all these years later. Alive. Free. Independent. Daring.

In the morning, Danny got up and left with a brief goodbye. He wished her well, and a long and happy marriage.

Jennifer knocked on her door after Danny had left. She wanted to know all the details. Alison couldn't remember them all. Over breakfast – lots of black coffee for Alison – she asked

Jennifer to help her keep her secret. Jennifer agreed. Of course she would. What happened in the Owen hotel would stay in the Owen hotel. Jennifer admitted to being slightly envious. Danny was a "good-looking boy". Jennifer said he obviously preferred short, plump, blonde-haired women to tall, slim, black-haired women. Alison laughed; they both laughed. 'Less of the plump,' said Alison. 'I have slimmed down to a size twelve for this wedding.' Then she burst into tears, and Jennifer spent the rest of the breakfast reassuring her that it was OK. She hadn't done anything terrible. It was perfectly understandable. She was a woman. A young woman about to get married. She wouldn't be the first, bride or groom alike, to have a last-minute one night stand. And nobody, but nobody, need ever know about Alison's encounter with Danny Boy. It was their secret. Forever.

April Fool

Jennifer awoke early: uncomfortable, hot, back aching. The dawn chorus was in full swing. She had never really taken much notice of the dawn chorus, but now that she preferred an open window all night, the bird song poured into her room every morning. There was something reassuring about the wonderful noise. A cacophony on the wing. Why did she keep thinking up these poetic thoughts? Was it her pregnant brain?

Her heart sank when she recalled all that had gone on yesterday. Marnie, turning up, out of the blue... she never thought she would see her. Ever. Yet there she was. A living, breathing, upset, angry, and pregnant, girl. Young woman. Woman. Somehow, Jennifer had never entertained the idea that the baby she had carried but wanted rid of straight away would one day be a grown woman. And how beautiful she would become. She had rarely thought about her daughter at all. Her life's secret. Not even her best friend (her former best friend) knew about Marnie. Nobody knew. She thought she had tucked that secret away for ever. But yesterday it had showed up at her door.

Did she regret it? Giving her away? Yes and no. Given her disastrous marriage to the vile Patrick – who may well have assaulted Marnie too – it had perhaps been the right decision. But of course she hadn't known Patrick at the time; let alone known how abusive he would prove to be. Even so, Marnie had been spared that. Or was she merely trying to self-justify giving up her baby?

She rubbed her tummy. She swore the bump grew bigger daily; which, she supposed, it did. Of course. What was she thinking? Baby brain again.

And Marnie pregnant too... Jennifer, a grandmother?! Of sorts. Perhaps Marnie wouldn't want Jennifer in her child's life. Jennifer understood that.

Yesterday had been... difficult. Had she done the right thing? It wasn't always easy to do the right thing, and sometimes it wasn't easy to know what the right thing was. Alison had once called her "hard-nosed". Jennifer, Alison had maintained, could be one of those millionaire business-women on *Dragon's Den*. She had that type of personality. That sharp edge. Jennifer told her she was not a business-woman. She wouldn't have a clue. Alison said she was missing her point. Jennifer wasn't sure, then, what the point was. But she knew now, maybe. She was hard. Very hard. Only a hard woman could give up her baby. Completely walk away. Only a diamond-hard woman could do that twice.

Jennifer sat up. Jake, lying on the floor alongside her bed as he always did, poked his head up and looked at her. She tapped the bed and he leaped up and on to it and sprawled across her feet. Jennifer checked her phone: 5:09. Too early for a coffee? She had cut down on caffeine, but couldn't bear to cut it out entirely. So she allowed herself one mug, every morning. Her treat. It made her feel a little more normal.

She was just about twenty-nine weeks pregnant. In the "safety zone"... her baby would probably survive if born now. She kind of hoped it would be... but not really. That was selfish. She wanted a healthy baby. She wanted her figure back too. Her lithe, slender body was unrecognisable. At her age, would it "spring back"? As some of the pregnancy books claimed it would? Stupid. Of course it wouldn't spring back. She would have to work at it. Work hard. She was still using her home gym, but taking it easy. Her back gave her too much gyp. She was having physio, had simple exercises to do. She hoped they would help.

It wasn't too early for coffee. She pushed back her duvet. Jake followed her downstairs. She entered the kitchen.

'Morning!' said Marnie.

She had her wavy dark brown hair messily tied up, and wore a baggy black jumper and a pair of grey sweat shorts. Nothing on her feet. She was getting the barista machine started. Jennifer noticed a large black rose tattoo running from Marnie's thigh down to her ankle. It was quite beautiful.

Marnie wasn't sure how to use the machine, so Jennifer took over.

'Could you let Jake out for me?' said Jennifer as she prepared their coffees. 'The latch just goes up on the window and it will open.'

Jake had his customary sniff around the garden. Jennifer finished preparing coffee and they sat at the island.

'You can't sleep well either, then?' said Marnie.

'I fall asleep OK. I'm in bed quite early, for me, because I'm so tired by the end of the day. But I wake up early these days and can't get back to sleep.'

'A bit like me.'

'When's your baby due, again?' Jennifer asked.

'At the end of July. Yours?'

'Around the end of June,' said Jennifer. 'A month or so ahead of you.'

'Wow. Amazing. So close... they will be niece and aunt.'

'I suppose they will be.'

'Weird.'

They sipped their coffee.

'Toast?' said Jennifer. She had never been big on bread but had craved it so far during the pregnancy. She made sure it was wholemeal, which she supposed was good for her. Better, at least.

'Oh, yes please!'

'Low fat spread or butter?'

'You got any olive spread?'

'I think so. Have a look in the fridge. Top shelf. Marmite?'

'Yes please.'

Jennifer busied herself with toast preparations. When Jake came back up to the French windows, Marnie slipped down from her stool and let him in. He licked her proffered hand, then circled his bed and settled down. He was a clever dog, and knew that he wouldn't get breakfast until eight o'clock. Jennifer was surprised to see how easily he had taken to Marnie. Since the Patrick days, Jake had been protective of Jennifer, and not very trusting of anybody new. But he seemed to trust Marnie. Perhaps Marnie was right, and he could sense she was... Jennifer didn't want to admit it, even to herself. This young woman was not her daughter, not really. She was a complete stranger. But of course Jake wouldn't understand this, wouldn't perceive things in these terms. He just trusted Marnie. She was in the pack.

Perhaps it was a sign? No. No, it wasn't. She couldn't afford to think like that.

Jennifer brought plates of toast to the island and watched as Marnie tucked into hers. She looked hungry. She finished her two slices quickly, and Jennifer offered to make more.

'Yes please. If you don't mind? I didn't eat much yesterday.'

'That's no good. You need to eat, especially at this time in your life.'

'I can give you some money for food...'

'No. Marnie. I need to say something. Listen, you stayed last night. That's fine. I couldn't have turned you out, pregnant as you are, and having travelled here. But... but you can't *stay* here.'

'Why can't I?'

Jennifer popped two more slices of bread into her posh toaster. The poor machine had never been so busy as it had these last few months.

'I'm not... I'm not really your mother, am I?'

'What are you then?'

Marnie was good at asking the simple yet profound questions. What indeed was she?

'I gave birth to you and gave you up for adoption. We went through this yesterday.'

'An adoption that never happened. A foster family who were just about good enough. Eventually. But my dad has long been gone off with another woman, my mum is dead and my sister hates me. I lived in children's homes, I lived with other foster carers. I just want to belong. Do you know how that feels?'

She knew. More than she had ever admitted to herself, let alone anybody else. But she wasn't going to admit that now.

'I can imagine,' Jennifer said.

'If I can't belong to you, who can I belong to?'

There really was no answer to that. Jennifer sighed. The toaster popped. Jennifer prepared the toast and took it to the island for Marnie.

'Eat up,' said Jennifer.

'I'm not an April fool, you know,' said Marnie. 'I really am your daughter. You just have to look at us to see that.'

'I know. You're very pretty.'

'Like you.'

'I once was.'

'You still are!'

'Thank you, Marnie. And you're right, you're not a fool. But maybe I am.'

Helena II

Alison made three different sorts of biscuits on Sunday afternoon: the crispy chocolate ones Helena was so fond of, as well as shortbread and ginger snaps. Ethan and Malcolm had picked at them, as had she, then she had popped them into her prettiest tin and hidden it away.

Now it was Monday, and almost threatening to rain (did it always rain when Helena visited?) and Alison had laid out the tea tray ready. Her best crockery today, the stuff she kept in the "buffet", untouched for most of the year. Christmas crockery, really. It might cheer Helena up. Perhaps it would cheer Alison up too.

Ethan had gone quiet on her... not exactly ignoring her... but not starting conversations. He hadn't offered her a hug for ages. Spontaneous hugging was something he'd always done. Affectionate and warm, that was Ethan. Always had been. Until now.

Damn Jennifer! Damn her to hell. She had destroyed not only their friendship, and that was bad enough, but also she had quite possibly destroyed Alison's relationship with her only child. It was unforgivable.

Alison spent the morning doing three loads of laundry. The threatened rain had not yet materialised, and it was a blowy day, so out it all went. It was wise to save money.

At half past one the doorbell dinged. Alison stopped at the hall mirror to smooth down her hair. It needed a cut, really. And she was developing a few greys, she had noticed over the Easter weekend. Luckily, with her ash blonde hair, they didn't really show. But nonetheless, they were unwelcome.

Had Helena gained weight? Perhaps she was comfort eating. The poor girl. She lumbered into the hall, and, as usual, she failed to remove her shoes before going into the lounge. This annoyed Alison. It was rude behaviour. Their's was an outdoor-shoe-removal household and Helena knew this. She had visited enough times, and had taken off her shoes, Alison recalled, whenever she was with Ethan. Perhaps she had merely copied him.

'Are you all right?' Alison asked, following Helena into the lounge.

'Not really,' said Helena.

The girl flopped herself on to the sofa. Malcolm's end.

'What's up?'

'What do you think?'

'I know, love. Let me fetch the tea tray. I've made biscuits for you.'

Alison left Helena in the lounge and prepared their refreshments in the kitchen. It started to rain, right on cue. 'Blast!' she called through to Helena. 'It's just started to rain! I'll go and grab the washing!'

The wind had got up too and the rain started to pelt down as Alison was halfway through getting in the laundry. She plucked the last item from the second of her lines, and picked up the laden basket and turned back towards the kitchen. Helena was standing at the sink, watching Alison struggle. *Really, she could have helped!*

Alison stuffed half of the damp laundry into the tumble dryer. Helena sloped back into the lounge. What a sullen girl she could be. That made two of them, Alison thought. She finished preparing the tea tray, and retrieved the hidden biscuit tin. She remembered her mistake the first time Helena had visited, and decanted a few biscuits on to a serving plate. She arranged everything artfully on her tray, and carried it through to the lounge.

She perched again at Malcolm's end of the sofa, and passed Helena her prettiest mug. She had found it a couple of years ago at a car boot sale. Helena took it with a muttered 'Thanks' and grabbed a couple of biscuits; both of which she proceeded to dunk into her tea. Alison quickly looked away. Dunking was one of Malcolm's most disconcerting habits. Not only disconcerting: it was absolutely disgusting.

Helena had barely uttered a word by the time she had finished her tea and eaten a total of five biscuits. *Comfort eating.* Alison understood. Lord knows she did that herself with chocolate. Her great weakness. 'More tea?' said Alison, trying to sound bright.

'Maybe in a bit,' said Helena.

'How is college?'

'Awful.'

'I'm sorry to hear that.'

'Everyone knows about your son.'

'What do you mean?'

'They know he's going to have a baby with That Woman.'

'I see. Well, not strictly "with"... that woman... she has declared her intention of going it alone.'

'How could he?'

'I don't know, Helena.'

'How could she?'

'Now, that I really don't know. She's always been... loose.'

'A tart, you mean.'

'Not so much a tart. Just rather fond of men.'

'She stole my boyfriend. I'll never forgive her. Will you?'

'For doing what she did with Ethan? No. Never. It's unforgivable.'

'My mum says it's wicked.'

Alison vaguely recalled Ethan telling her that Helena's family were religious. Church-goers. Helena not so much, she thought he'd said.

'I've prayed for Ethan's soul,' said Helena.

Alison crossed and uncrossed her legs. 'Have you?'

'And that woman's. Jezebel.'

'Je*nnifer*.'

'Whatever. She is the worst kind of woman. Ethan is the worst kind of man.'

'Boy.'

Alison got up to make more tea. Helena had every right to feel betrayed. Didn't she? But the religious turn in the conversation made her uncomfortable. She was not a believer, not really. Never had been. Helena was laying it on a bit thick. Surely she and Ethan had... slept together? Hadn't they? Or had she simply made that assumption? Still, the poor girl was hurt, and Alison knew only too well how that felt.

As the kettle boiled, she again retrieved the biscuit tin and this time she took it through to the lounge. The conversation became lighter, less religious. Helena talked about her plans for after college. She was going to look for a job, she said. She was going to look for a new boyfriend.

Only after Helena had gone, after a second cup of tea and half a dozen more biscuits, did Alison realise that neither of them had mentioned the most important person in all of this "hot mess", as Helena called it. They had whined about Ethan, whined about Jennifer, talked about themselves as victims. Yet Alison had not enjoyed the visit. She didn't actually enjoy Helena's company at all. What had Ethan seen in her, truly?

And that little person, unborn, all the troubles of the world waiting for him, they had not discussed.

Why should they? Alison asked herself as she washed up the cups and plates, the spoons. Why should either of them concern themselves with that... baby. *It's a baby, Alison.* Malcolm had said this to her only last night as they were getting ready for bed. *And not only a baby. Our grandchild.*

After washing up, Alison smoked another secret cigarette in the back garden. She couldn't afford to let this become a habit, she told herself.

Ethan got home from college at four. Alison made him a coffee and offered the biscuit tin. He didn't dunk his biscuits; never had. Before she knew what she was saying— 'I do wish Helena wasn't a dunker!'

'What do you mean?'

'Oh. Well, she popped round for tea earlier and I noticed she dunked her biscuits.'

'Why did she come round? Did you invite her?'

Did she? No. She didn't.

'Don't tell me. She invited herself?'

'Yes.' A text letting Alison know she was popping round. Not even a question.

'Typical of her. She's a taker, Mum.'

'A taker?'

'Scrounger. You give an inch and she'll take a mile. That kind of person.'

'I see.'

'Why would you have her round here?'

'She's done nothing wrong, Ethan. She's hurt.'

Ethan rolled his eyes.

'She is! And she has every right to be.'

'She likes to play the victim.'

'She *is* a victim.'

'Of what? She was my sort-of girlfriend. Kept saying she wanted to be, but she would never... you know. It wasn't a proper boyfriend-girlfriend-thing. We never actually...'

'I see. I did wonder. She comes from a religious family, doesn't she?'

'They're religious when they want to be.'

'Ah.'

'I didn't like them much. In the end I didn't like her much.'

'So you had this... fling... with your Aunty Jennifer because Helena wouldn't... you know.'

'Not really. And she's not my aunt. It just happened. That's all. There is no explanation. It just happened.'

'Sounds a bit feeble.'

'Jennifer is... Mum, she's fun. She's good to be around.'

'Is she?'

'Yes! You know that. You've been friends long enough.'

'We were "friends" for too long and not any more.'

'Mum. Can't you rethink all this?'

'Rethink what?'

'All this anger. I know this situation isn't ideal. None of it. But at the core of all this there is a baby. An innocent little baby. That's all that matters.'

'You sound like your father.'

'He's right. I'm right.'

'I can't forgive her, Ethan. She betrayed my trust.'

'How?'

'Do I need to spell it out?'

'If I was fifteen, you'd be right. Even if I was seventeen, you would have a point. But I'm eighteen, Mum, an adult. It was one consenting adult with another consenting adult. There is no crime, no indecency—'

'Plenty of indecency! She was your aunt.'

'No, she wasn't. Isn't.'

'She behaved like an aunt. Until she didn't.'

'Yes, I suppose that's true. But she didn't exactly force me, Mum. You know what I'm saying, don't you?'

Alison had to look away. Certain images she did not want to see. 'She's old enough to be your mother. She watched you grow up. On and off. She was in a position of trust.'

'Not really. She was a free agent. So was I. The age gap doesn't matter when it's all just fun. We were two adults. That's it, Mum.'

'It's a little bit more that just "fun" now though, isn't it?'

'Yes.'

'It's all become rather serious. You're lumbered, Ethan, at your age. She trapped you!'

'What are you on about?'

'She did this on purpose.'

'She did not. You've got that wrong. She is shocked. Totally shocked. She had no idea she was going to get pregnant.'

'That's what she says. She's a consummate liar.'

'I don't think so. She's always been very honest and open with me.'

'Oh, please.'

'I tell you who is a liar. Helena.'

'She is not.'

'She is. It's not a good idea for you to keep seeing her, Mum. I wish you wouldn't. She really is a scrounger.'

'You're telling me who I can and can't choose as a friend?!'

'No. I'm just saying you have a true friend in Jennifer. She needs you. I know she won't admit that, or ever ask for help, but she's all alone with this and I know she would appreciate your support. She doesn't want my help, I get that. She's understanding of my feelings. My age. She's generous.'

'Evidently.'

Ethan got up. 'You know what I mean. She's being very fair about everything.'

'Easy to be fair when you have pots of money and a big house and you take advantage of a nice boy.'

'Listen to yourself! I can't talk to you when you're like this.'

'Like what?'

'Irrational. Weird. Mean.'

'Where are you going?'

'I'm going to see Jennifer. See if she needs anything. Check in. You know? That thing that friends do?'

Ethan, meet Marnie

Jennifer was outside, around the side of the house, chatting to Scott about the garden. He always had lots of ideas that he was keen to discuss with her. But this time she had an idea of her own: a wild garden. A small pond, a little meadow, native plants aplenty. Nest boxes nailed to trees, attached to the side of the house. She enjoyed the tidy view from the kitchen-diner-lounge's French windows: the neat lawn, the carefully planned and tended borders. But it wasn't particularly good for wildlife, she had come to understand, and she wanted to do her bit. It would be nice for her child to have wildlife in their garden. Not just birds, but frogs, toads, newts, dragon flies. And lots of nice-smelling plants. Sensory. Scott was keen. It was his kind of gardening, he said. Lavender, mint, rosemary, all would smell divine over the summer. Stocks. Hyacinths in the spring. She wanted native flowers, like hollyhocks and foxgloves. A log pile for insects would be easy to achieve too. So, Jennifer had decided that the space around to the side, on the right of the house, would be the wild patch. Scott would sort it all out.

'We'll start with a pond liner,' he said. 'Not too big? Although you do have the room for a biggish pond.'

'Not too *deep*. I suppose we would need to fence it all off? It might look rather nice anyway. The scruffy part fenced off. But

I don't want my sprog— ooh! Bad word. I don't want my baby falling in either.'

'Of course. I can build a fence. Would you like a gate?'

'Better had.'

'Sure.'

When Marnie wandered out into the garden, clutching a mug of ginger tea, wearing scruffy walking boots, shorts, a baggy pink jumper, and messy up-do hair, Scott didn't bat an eyelid. He must have noticed the tattoo. He must have noticed the pregnancy bump. Jake loped over to Marnie. He did seem very taken with her.

'Scott, this is Marnie. She's staying with me for... for a few days.'

'Right. Hi, Marnie.'

Then, to all their surprise, Ethan wandered around the corner of the house. He stopped, and his gaze travelled to and from all three of them in turn. 'I heard your voices,' Ethan said. Jake barked, once, a small hello. Ethan made a fuss of him, and once he was satisfied, Jake returned to Marnie.

'Come on over, Ethan,' said Jennifer. 'We're just discussing a wildlife garden. I need to do my bit. You've met Scott before, haven't you?'

'Sure. Sort of. We've waved. Hi, Scott.'

'Scott, this is Ethan. He's my best friend's son.'

If Scott knew or understood more, he didn't let on. Not a flicker. Jennifer suspected he did know, all of it. Everything. Probably he had even worked out who Marnie might be. Ethan clearly hadn't. Why would he? He was staring at her. His eyes lingered on the tattoo. Her bump was fairly obvious, but it was small and neat.

'Ethan,' said Jennifer. 'This is Marnie. Marnie, this is Ethan. I've known him all his life.' *Why did she say that?* 'I'm his aunt in all but blood.'

'Hi,' said Marnie. She took a sip of her ginger tea.

'Hi,' said Ethan. 'Did you two meet at... antenatal classes?' He had noticed the bump, then.

'No,' said Jennifer. 'I don't go to classes. Not my thing.'

'We could go though, couldn't we?' said Marnie, looking eagerly at Jennifer. 'Together?'

Ethan and Scott exchanged the briefest of confused looks.

'We'll see,' said Jennifer. It started to spit with rain. 'Let's go indoors. Would you like a tea or a coffee, Scott?'

'No, thank you. I'll do a few measurements out here then work out what I need for the fence and so on. And you want a row of nest boxes for sparrows?'

'Yes. Whatever will work.'

'No problem. I'll get it all bought on Thursday morning then make a start.'

'Take my credit card.'

Jennifer made drinks for herself, Marnie, and Ethan, and they all sat at the kitchen island.

'How's your mum?' asked Jennifer.

'Weird,' said Ethan.

'I see.'

'Hanging out with Helena.'

'*The* Helena?'

'Yes.'

'Why?'

'She thinks they have become friends.'

'And have they?'

Ethan shrugged. Marnie, confused, looked from one to the other.

Jennifer raised her eyebrows at Ethan. He shrugged, again. He was remarkably good at shrugging. Somehow he managed to make his shrugs say exactly what he meant. Jennifer then raised her eyebrows at Marnie, who didn't shrug. She didn't seem to respond at all. She looked confused. Since when had life descended into such a soap opera?

'Do you know who I might be?' said Marnie to Ethan.

'Jennifer's... friend?'

'Not really.'

Jennifer cleared her throat. Both of the youngsters, and Jake, turned to her. Jake's tail wagged in slow expectation. She had often thought he understood every word she ever uttered. 'Ethan, Marnie is my daughter.'

'Oh. Right. Wow... but what daughter?'

'Her only daughter. Although there might be another on the way. I'd quite like a baby sister.'

'I ... I wanted her to have the best life... so I give her up for adoption.'

'Except I didn't have the best life and I was never adopted. Go figure.'

Ethan's mouth fell open. He looked from one woman to the other and back again. Dozy boy. Always had been. Nice, but dozy. Was the penny even dropping?

'Does Mum know?'

'No. I think it needs to stay that way. For now.' Jennifer turned to Marnie. 'Ethan's mum and I are best friends. Were. We seem to have fallen out.'

'Why?'

Ethan looked uncomfortable. Jake, losing interest, had retired to his bed by the French windows. It looked rather inviting. Jennifer wanted to join him there, basking in the sun which had now come out after the shower.

'We had a disagreement,' said Jennifer.

'That's just another word for falling out. What did you disagree *about*? And did you really not tell her about me? You didn't tell your best friend? Why not?'

Marnie was close to tears. Ethan looked terrified.

'We weren't best friends at the time. We've been up and down, over the years, in and out of touch sometimes. That was an out-of-touch time. That's all.'

'That's all?'

'Yes. Look. Marnie. I may as well tell you the tru—'

'No,' said Ethan. 'I'll tell her. Mum and Jennifer haven't always got on. They're friends, but they're quite... different, you know? Almost like frenemies, sometimes. But this time they fell out because I'm the father of Jennifer's baby. Mum was upset. *Is* upset. She thinks it's all wrong.'

Now it was Marnie's turn to look from one to the other. Not as gormless as Ethan, though. Christ, she was quick-witted. Like her mother. Marnie *got* things. She really was her daughter. When Marnie burst into loud laughter, Jennifer wasn't entirely surprised. She was also relieved. Ethan smiled nervously.

'Well, that's refreshing,' said Jennifer.

Marnie laughed again. Ethan continued to smile, uncertain.

'It's funny,' said Marnie. 'My real mum is pregnant by a man young enough to be her son... you're younger than me, aren't you?'

'I'm eighteen.'

'God. I'm twenty-three. Wanna hazard a guess of the age of the father of *my* baby?'

Ethan considered. 'Twenty-eight?'

Marnie shook her head. 'Guess again.'

'Thirty-one?'

'You're going to take forever. So I'll just tell you. The father is fifty-two.'

Jennifer spat out her ginger tea.

SUMMER

It's Getting Hot in Here...

The age of her baby's father was the only thing Marnie was prepared to say about him, other than that he was "a jerk". He didn't know she was pregnant. He probably didn't even know who she was. She had a thing for older men, unsuitable men. Her love life was a disaster.

Like mother, like daughter, was Jennifer's secret thought. There was an odd sort of symmetry to it. Shouldn't it all be the other way around? Marnie's fifty-something walking disaster, this mystery man, should be the father of Jennifer's baby; Ethan, the not-mysterious (not *remotely* mysterious) teenager the father of Marnie's baby. But life rarely obeyed its own rules. If Jennifer had learned anything over the course of her existence, it was that. Life and its vagaries. Life and its spillages, its clumsiness. Anarchy.

Perhaps Alison would have remained her friend if the father of Jennifer's baby has been an older man; a respectable man; an *un*respectable man. A different man. Perhaps it was foolish to have blurted it out like that, to have given it all away. Jennifer would give anything, anything at all, to have her friend back. Difficult to admit, even to herself, but she missed her, every single day. She had tried more ringing; sent further friendly messages and invitations via Ethan. She had e-mailed again. But nothing. She saw more of Malc than she saw of

Alison. He had popped round a few times on his way home from work to see if there was anything she needed. Odd jobs. Fixing taps. Heavy lifting. Luckily, Scott had also proved to be helpful and kind, and he helped her out with that kind of work. But it was always good to see Malc. Jennifer calmly explained who Marnie was. He'd seemed surprised, like Ethan, but accepting. Jennifer asked them both not to tell Alison. Yet. Jennifer hoped she would one day get the chance to introduce Marnie herself. That was her preference. Malc and Ethan got it.

On Malc's last visit, Jennifer had asked, 'How's Alison doing?'

He had shaken his head sadly. 'She thinks she's doing fine.'

'Yes. I see.'

'She's spending time with that Helena girl. God knows why. She eats like a horse and she looks like one. A pregnant horse. Oh! Sorry.'

'No worries, Malc. You know I can take a joke. Not to mention a faux pas. But I wonder why she feels the need to entertain this girl?'

'God knows.'

'I recall I didn't think much to her. I met her on Christmas Day, if you remember?'

'I do remember. And did she eat like a horse?'

'Oh yes.'

'I think she's a nasty little thing, really. I wish Alison would dump her. She's not like your Marnie.'

Her Marnie? They were some way from that, Malc.

But Marnie had not yet left. The arrangement was still... temporary. Certain... difficult subjects were not discussed. Certain options were ignored. But each day came and went, and Marnie was still there. Her room – *the room she was using* – looked like a bombsite. To be fair, she did help to keep the kitchen clean, and she did her own laundry. Jennifer kept out of Marnie's room, mostly. Glanced in, occasionally. They took it in turns to walk Jake, and that was a godsend. Jennifer mostly took him out in the mornings when she felt at her most energetic. Marnie tended to take him out in the evenings. Sometimes they both took him out for the evening walk, if Jennifer's legs weren't too swollen. Swollen ankles! Unimaginable just a few months ago, but here they were. The ugliest of ankles. *Cankles*. She had taken to wearing long flowing trousers to cover them up. Long flowing shirts too. Nothing much felt comfortable. She couldn't wear heels, so instead wore trainers, or a pair of Birkenstock sandals; which, she had to admit to herself, and to Marnie, were very comfortable.

The summer was long and hot and dry. Day after day of sunny weather. Jennifer did her best not to complain. Marnie seemed to sail through the hot days, the sticky nights. Not so Jennifer. She was taking tepid showers, tepid baths. She used her gym equipment in the evenings, if she could be bothered to use it at all. She was getting bat wings.

Three weeks to D-day. Jennifer could not wait. The end of June couldn't come soon enough. Yet – she was scared. Terrified. She had bought almost all the stuff her baby would need. Enough for two babies. In her heart, Jennifer felt Marnie was there to stay. And it was all right. Jennifer's third bedroom was the nursery. Jennifer had furnished it with two cots, although Marnie had expressed the intention of co-sleeping, and breastfeeding. Jennifer had long-ago decided she would not breastfeed beyond the first two or three days. She couldn't bear the thought of it. Marnie would be the better mother.

Would it work? Any of it? Their relationship was... friendly. House-mate-like. Warm, often. But neither of them discussed "things" anymore. So much had become taboo. It all felt rather artificial. Doomed to fail. Marnie had stopped asking "Why?"

But there was no more talk of Marnie "moving on". No more mention of her leaving. Jennifer helped Marnie to pay off all that she owed on the flat, and the tenancy was terminated to everybody's satisfaction. And Marnie became increasingly ensconced in her room, in the house, in Jennifer's life.

And the great thing was that most of the time, they did get along well. Sometimes very well. They had the same sense of humour, so the quiet sharing of that was good for both of them. Jennifer tried to ignore the ever-present guilt; and bought everything that Marnie needed, and everything she might need, for her baby. Jennifer also bought things that would probably never be needed. It was one way she could make amends for giving Marnie up. Marnie accepted everything with a tacit grace.

Tragedy

'When was your due date again?' asked Marnie, tucking into a bowl of porridge, liberally laced with oatmilk, chopped banana, and dates. Both women had taken to eating odd meals at odd times. It was too hot, and they were too pregnant, to be bothered with cooking. Jennifer's fridge was rammed with fruit, vegetables, cheese, olives, meats, and oat milk for Marnie who was "aiming to be a vegan". Jennifer wondered if Marnie's heart was truly in it. She swore she was picking at the ham, the cocktail sausages. Definitely the cheese.

'The twenty-seventh of June.' Jennifer was eating a cheese and cucumber sandwich, on wholemeal bread, washed down with sparkling water. She was tired, bored, and impatient. And, alarmingly, hungry. All the time now. She had become a grazer. At least she was getting her five a day. She had expected to feel less hungry with her stomach squashed up by the ever-growing baby, but it hadn't worked out that way. Perhaps it was her body's way of ensuring she had energy for labour. She was dreading what was to come. At the same time, she couldn't wait. The baby's head had "engaged". She was keen to get out, just as Jennifer was keen to get her out.

'Four days late then,' said Marnie, shovelling into her mouth a spoonful of the porridge-banana-dates-oatmilk-combo.

'Yes, thank you. I've worked that one out.'

'Sorry.'

'No, don't be. I just wish it was over. My baby could be four days old by now. I might already be an expert at changing nappies.'

Nappies had proved to be a bone of contention. Marnie insisted they should be using washable cotton reusables. Jennifer favoured disposables. She had bought lots of packs of Pampers, and Marnie had tutted, muttered. In the end a compromise was reached: they would have both types in the house. So Jennifer bought a stack of reusables in different sizes. And she bought buckets. And sterilizer fluid. And bottles, and a different sort of bucket for those, and sterilizer fluid for that bucket. It was endless, the things you had to buy for a baby. Two babies. Little white onesies, cot and pram sheets and blankets. Jennifer, her generosity getting the better of her, had bought two beautiful Silver Cross prams, but modern ones. Prams that could later become strollers.

Marnie had bought nothing. She had no money. Jennifer suspected she owed money, besides the outstanding rent on her former flat ("room"), but it was not discussed. They had discussed other things. Marnie would get a job once her baby was a few months old. Then she would pay over some keep, pay her way. Jennifer had agreed. In the meantime, she was supporting Marnie. It was only right. Jennifer felt she owed her daughter. Quite a lot. This was a way to repay her. Jennifer had agreed to babysit Marnie's baby while Marnie worked. What kind of work was she after? Jennifer had asked. 'Dunno,' Marnie had replied. 'I've got no skills. Barely got any GCSEs.'

Jennifer was considering offering to help Marnie return to study, if she wanted to do that. But she hadn't yet discussed it with her. Perhaps she would do so after both babies were born. Seriously, they were going to have their work cut out for many

148

months. Many years. Jennifer, although inexperienced in motherhood, understood enough, had seen and witnessed enough, to know that for the first six months or so, life would be absolutely nothing but babies for both her and Marnie. In a strange way she was looking forward to it. It was going to be a profound bonding experience, she hoped. There was still quite a lot of bonding to do. Jennifer suspected they hadn't even really begun...

Marnie finished her porridge. 'Shall I take Jake out for his walk?' she said. 'You look knackered.'

'Yes, please. I am rather shattered.'

'Go and put your feet up and I'll fix you a cold drink when I get back.'

How Jennifer longed for a glass of very cold dry white wine. She had champagne in the fridge, two bottles, all ready and waiting to toast the birth of her baby. She anticipated visitors. She had already mentioned it to Scott and Kimberley. They had both agreed it would be wonderful to have a glass to "wet the baby's head", as Scott put it. Kimberley was proving to be an absolute godsend, coming in every week now to clean the house. Scott was keeping the garden looking beautiful. The wildlife area was coming on a treat. The pond was *in situ* and already attracting insects and birds.

Ethan and Malcolm would want to celebrate. Perhaps even Alison? Surely she would... rally? Come round? Cave in? Be curious, if nothing else? This baby was her grandchild. They would be family, of sorts, related by blood. More than friends. It was an odd thought, and, Jennifer knew – feared – it was a bad thought for Alison. She had heard nothing from her since February; four months. It was hurtful. But she understood. The friendship had been pushed to breaking point and – snap! – it had broken.

Marnie pulled on her boots, and fetched Jake's lead and a

couple of poop bags from the cupboard in the kitchen. Jake, excited, flitted heavily around her as she prepared for their walk. Jennifer waddled – waddled! – to the kitchen sofa. The real-life living room. The large, actual, living room at the front of the house was rarely used by either of them. It was more convenient to flop on to the sofa in the kitchen after eating. Or, increasingly, it was easier to flop on to it *while* eating. Jennifer had always been a stickler for eating at the table, or at the island. Not eating on sofas. She was no slob. But that rule was now broken. And, like the living room, the dining room was also pretty much unused. Indeed it had rarely ever been used, the island proving itself perfectly adequate for Jennifer's mostly solo dining. The dining room was now a storage space for the prams, boxes of nappies, baby gyms. Nursery over- spill. The nursery itself was all done, ready and waiting for its tiny new occupants.

Jennifer woke with a start. Her phone. Ringing. She struggled to her feet (like all her sofas, the kitchen sofa was luxuriously deep) and waddled to the island. She rooted around in her powder-blue Aspinal bag – her latest treat to herself – and retrieved her phone. She noticed the time. Had Marnie really been gone for an hour and a half? It was still so hot.

It was Marnie calling. Jennifer put the phone on speaker. 'Hello?' she said.

'Mum!'

'What's the matter?'

'It's all my fault!' Marnie sobbed.

Jennifer felt a shiver down her spine. She felt cold. 'What's happened?'

'It's Jake. He ran off... there was another dog. Barking. He just slipped away from me. Mum!'

Jennifer heard a man's voice in the background.

Then he spoke on the phone. 'Are you the dog owner?'

'Yes. What the hell has happened?'

'My brother's in a bit of a state. There was nothing he could do. I'm driving because he can't. He's... he's rather shaken up.'

'Has my dog been run over?'

'Yes. That's it. I'm afraid so.'

'Can a vet be called?'

'Already tried that. They won't come out, but we can take him ourselves. So we are doing that now.'

'Is Marnie with you then? My daughter?'

'Yes. Yes, she is. She's holding up the phone so I can speak to you. It doesn't look good, I'm afraid.'

'Oh god. Which vet are you going to?'

'Atkinsons.'

'That's my vet. They know Jake.'

'I'm afraid he's dead. I'm pretty certain he's dead. Or nearly dead.'

'I had the feeling you were going to say that.'

Marnie wailing in the background. The sound of the car. The man's calm, soothing voice. No sound from Jake. No whimpering. Just Marnie's sobs, the hum of the car engine.

'We're almost there,' said the man.

'I'll be there too. Five minutes.'

'OK. I'm truly sorry.'

Jake was nearly dead. A faint heartbeat, the vet said. Severe injuries. Lots of broken bones. Probably internal injuries. No hope. He would probably die overnight. There was so much blood. Jennifer barely noticed. She held him, her boy, while the vet gave him the injection. She rocked him, told him she loved him, and hoped he could hear. Somehow he could, she thought.

Later, she emerged into the waiting room. Waiting for her

were Marnie and the man who had carried Jake into the vets, which had been on the verge of closing for the day. Now everybody else had gone.

'He's gone,' said Jennifer. 'He's dead. The vet put him down.' She couldn't look at Marnie.

'I am sorry,' said the man. He had a kind face. He must be a strong man. Jake weighed a ton.

'Thank you for helping,' said Jennifer.

'Not at all. My brother is going to be devastated. There really was nothing he could have done. Your dog just flew at us, out of nowhere.'

'He never runs away. Never.' Jennifer looked firmly at the man.

'I think your daughter said there was another dog...'

'It was barking at Jake,' said Marnie. 'Jake barked back. This other dog was really aggressive. Next thing... I just couldn't hold him.'

'He never runs away,' said Jennifer to the kind strong man. 'Never did. Not even when he was a puppy.'

Marnie sobbed, and ran from the waiting room. Jennifer didn't go after her.

'Can I give you a lift home?' said the man.

'No, I have my car. Could you put him on the back seat for me? I'm taking him home. I'm going to bury him in the garden.'

'Of course.'

Jennifer left the building, and was submerged into the hot evening. She saw the driver. She ignored him. He ignored her. Pretended not to see her. Seemed to sink down in the passenger seat of his car, staring at his mobile phone. Good for him that he had a strong brother. This kind man laid Jake on the back seat of Jennifer's car. Jake was wrapped in a blanket, and the nurse had cleaned him up. But there was still a lot of blood.

'Look, are you sure you are able to drive?' said the man.

How old-fashioned he was! Oddly so. Posh. But who cared? Jake was dead.

'I'm fine, really. Thank you.'

'I'm not sure where your daughter went.'

'To hell, for all I care.'

'Oh, wait a moment—'

'No. Thank you. He was the best-behaved dog. He never slipped his lead, never wrenched himself away. She's lying.'

'But I saw—'

'I have to go now. Thanks for your help. Please tell your brother I don't blame him. I don't want to speak to him, but I don't blame him.'

'I understand. Will you be all right getting your dog out when you get home?'

'Yes, thank you. I have help there.'

'Got it.'

Was that a hint of disappointment? His knight in shining armour act thwarted?

'Again, I'm deeply sorry,' he said. 'It's a cruel loss. And not great timing, I'm sure.' He glanced at her belly.

Jennifer thanked him once more; then she got into her car, and pulled out of the car park. She wasn't entirely surprised when she saw the kind man following her. The car must be damaged. She hadn't even looked. Couldn't. There would be an insurance claim; and a vet bill. She would deal with those later. For now, it was her and Jake, alone.

The Phone Call II

When she pulled on to the drive, she realised there was not a chance in hell of her single-handedly getting Jake out of her car and round into the garden. She would need to ask Scott. Perhaps she shouldn't. It wouldn't be fair on him. He did so much for her already. Yes, she paid him well for all his work, but even so, he wasn't a servant.

She rummaged in her bag. Got blood on it. That was the end of the expensive bag, but that thought came and went with barely a ripple. She had blood on her hands. Jake's blood. It was no different to her own. She trembled, wiped her hands on her slacks, took out her mobile phone. She found the number she wanted.

'Ethan? Can you come? No, it's not that. Don't panic. It's Jake. He's dead. He's in my car. I can't lift him out. It's Marnie's fault. She didn't look after him properly... I don't know... I don't much care... Can you help me bury Jake? Thanks, Ethan. See you in a bit.'

Alison looked up from her cross stitch. She was getting an hour in on this project (dusty-ancient, hanging-around, regretfully-boring, old-fashioned) before starting on their evening meal. Ethan had been lounging on the sofa, sort-of-chatting to her (not that he ever really said much these days). Listlessly he'd made them both a cup of tea. Then his phone rang, and she heard, "Oh, hello, Jennifer..." Then Ethan sounded stressed, dismayed. He ended the call.

'Everything all right?' said Alison. The baby was due around now, she thought. Who was she kidding? She *knew*. Surely Ethan wasn't expected to be holding Jennifer's hand and mopping her brow?

Ethan stood. 'Where's Dad?'

'He's in the garden. Hiding in the shed, I expect. Doing a crossword. You know what he's like.'

'We need to go over to Aunty Jennifer's.'

'Do you have to keep calling her that? It's inappropriate now.'

'Whatever, Mum. Aren't you in the least bit curious? Listen to yourself! Jake's been killed. He's been knocked down by a car. Jennifer's distraught. She needs help burying him.'

'Can't that gardener chap do it? Scott or whatever his name is.'

'Mum!'

'Well, she pays him to be her odd job man, doesn't she?'

'That's not the point. She needs... a friend. Her friends. I'll go get Dad.'

Alison felt her face turn red. She put down her cross stitch. Poor Jake. Poor Jen— No. She wouldn't go there. Maybe this was some kind of karma. She and Helena had been discussing karma only last week. Helena visited most weeks now. When Ethan was at his part-time summer job. His *McJob* as Helena described it, scathing; and, Alison had noticed, condescending. Helena didn't have a job at all, but Alison had not brought that up. She didn't want to fall out with the girl.

Alison went into the kitchen as Ethan and Malcolm came in the back door with shovels and spades. A big piece of sack, or something, too. Malcolm was always resourceful.

'Are you coming with us, Alison?' Malcolm said.

'No. Of course not.'

'Alison...'

'What?'

'Hasn't this gone on long enough?' said Malcolm. Ethan had reached the front door, and was holding it open for his dad.

'Malcolm, this will never end. For me. You know how I feel about her. What she did.'

Malcolm reached the front door.

'What about your tea?' said Alison.

'What about it?'

'What shall I make for you? When?'

'Sort yourself out, Alison...' and there was a meaning in those words she didn't like. She wasn't sure quite what Malcolm was getting at, or if he was getting at anything at all. He was difficult to read nowadays. 'I mean, get your own tea. We'll grab chips or something later. Come on, son.'

And they were gone, and the house was silent, and Alison felt... reproached. Inferior. Alone. But she would not go. Ever again. She would never again speak to Jennifer, no matter what. She heard the car start. She heard it speed off. Fast, for Malcolm, the most careful of drivers.

Why did they care so much about... That Woman? *Why?*

Poor Jake, though. He had been such a lovely dog. He didn't deserve this.

Burial

Jennifer opened the door. She almost fell into Malcolm's arms. She couldn't help it. She was not one for showing any emotions, usually; other than a simple, low-level sort of contentment; but this time it couldn't be helped. Tears would flow, as Jake's blood had flowed.

Alison hadn't come with them. And this made Jennifer cry all the more. She had hoped... she had *hoped*. Just as she'd hoped all through this pregnancy that Alison would come round, thaw out, chill out, and want to be involved. Alison knew what Jake meant to her. How he had protected her from Patrick. At first Alison had not believed how vile Patrick had been; but once she had understood, at least about the emotional abuse, she seemed to get it. Jennifer had never let on that he had also physically harmed her. She'd told Alison about the name-calling, the gas-lighting, the affairs. And Alison had loved Jake too, in her own rather distant way. Jake had always licked Alison's hands calmly, accepting; he'd never seen her as a threat.

Ethan was carrying implements and what looked like a sack. To put Jake in. Of course. Good thinking. She'd rather lost her head, gone to pieces. But she had implements here, garden tools that Scott kept neatly stored and locked up in a shed at the bottom of the garden. But it was the sort of thing Malcolm, and Ethan, would have thought of. They were good like that. Malcolm was ever-practical, and it was rubbing off on Ethan. Alison was a lucky woman.

'I'm sorry, Jennifer,' Malcolm said.

'Thanks, Malc.'

'Where's Jake?'

'In the back of my car. I can't lift him...'

'Of course not. We'll get him out. Where would you like him buried?'

'I think in my wild garden? Would that work, do you think?'

'Of course, that would be perfect. Wouldn't it, Ethan?'

'Sure,' said Ethan.

'Come on then, lad, let's go get him. We'll take him straight round the side, Jennifer. We thought we could lay him in this sacking.'

'Thanks, Malc. Really. Thank you.'

She made them tea, and brought it out on a tray. Jake lay next to his grave, still and silent. Malcolm and Ethan were sweating. Ethan had removed his shirt. She registered this as a plain fact, nothing more.

'How deep, d'you reckon?' said Malcolm, taking his mug of tea from the tray. 'Oh, thanks, Jennifer. Just the job.'

'It's the least I can do,' said Jennifer. 'Well, he's a big dog. I don't know. Three feet or so? He's got to be properly buried.'

'That was my thinking. Maybe we'll go four. Keep digging, Ethan.'

Ethan nodded, and dug a bit more, before pausing for his tea too. The sun was just dipping behind the trees that lined that side of the garden. That would be a bit cooler for them, Jennifer thought.

Once they had drank their tea, she put the tray on the bench by the wall of the house and she went to Jake. She crouched beside him, stroked his head, and spoke to him. It felt right. The right thing to do. She felt her belly tighten. Hard, for quite a while. The strongest Braxton-Hicks yet. She ignored it.

Later, Malcolm and Ethan laid the sack cloth in the grave. They lifted Jake. Jennifer kissed him one last time. The men lowered him into his resting place.

'Do you want to say a few words?' said Malcolm. Ethan put his T-shirt back on, and stood respectfully alongside the grave.

'Yes, I think I do. Jake, you were the best... the best of dogs. *My* best. The loveliest boy. I had you for ten amazing years. Thank you. Rest easy now, and enjoy your walks and ball chasing for ever more, in your special place. Wherever that is. Good bye, lovely Jake.'

Malcolm swept a tear from his face. Ethan coughed.

'All right, Jennifer?' said Malcolm. 'Why don't you go inside and put your feet up. We'll finish here.'

Of course, Malcolm knew she shouldn't see Jake buried. He was ever-kind, super-sensible. She took the tea tray back into the kitchen, and reflected on how lucky her baby would be to have such a flipping brilliant grandfather. Because Malcolm would step into that role, of that she had no doubt. He was born for it. But would her baby girl have a grandmother?

She couldn't think about that now. It was down to Alison, anyway.

Half an hour later, the menfolk trundled into the kitchen, looking hot and tired.

'All done,' said Malcolm. 'We've made the mound as neat as we can.'

'I think I'll scatter more wild flower seeds on it. See what Jake gives me next summer.'

'That's a lovely idea, Jennifer.'

'Doing my bit for nature, you know? I've seen quite a few butterflies. Jake… Jake's body will nourish the soil, won't it?'

'Oh, yes. Nothing is ever wasted in nature.'

It was comforting. 'Can I buy you two something to eat? You've worked your arses off.'

Malcolm looked at Ethan who nodded.

'Chinese?' said Jennifer.

'Perfect,' said Malcolm.

The chow mein, egg fried rice, and spring rolls were devoured rapidly, appreciatively, by Malcolm and Ethan. Jennifer, appetite lost, pushed hers around her plate. She nibbled at some rice, but her heart wasn't in it. When Ethan offered to finish her plate for her, she pushed it over to him.

'Where's Marnie gone then?' said Ethan.

'I don't know,' said Jennifer. 'I can't worry about that too much right now. She's the sort of young woman who always has somewhere to go.'

'Yeah,' said Ethan. Perhaps he didn't quite know what she meant. He was oddly naive, at times.

'Ah,' said Malcolm. He knew exactly what she meant. Of course. He gave the impression of innocence, unawareness, unworldliness. But it was a false impression. Malcolm was clued-up. Jennifer studied him now as he finished his food. Kind face, as ever. He'd been the same at school. Patience personified. For the first time, and she knew this was a failing on her part, she had an insight into what Alison saw in him.

Yellow Roses

Jennifer woke to the sound of her doorbell. The mellifluous chimes. She hauled herself from bed, having a strong Braxton-Hicks, and made her slow way down the stairs. The chimes burst into life again.

'All right!' she shouted. 'I'm on my way!'

She opened the door to the kind man from yesterday. He was holding a huge bunch of flowers – yellow roses.

'I'm sorry if I disturbed you,' he said. 'I felt I ought to call and check you're all right. And bring you these. They're from my brother.'

'Oh.' She took the flowers, smelled their sweet, dew-droppy smell. 'Thank you.'

'Are you all right?'

'No, not really.'

'You got your dog buried OK?'

'Yes. Some friends helped me.'

'Friends. Good. That's good. I hated the thought of you trying to dig a grave. I have to confess to following you yesterday.'

'I know. I saw. I didn't mind.'

'I'm not a crazy stalker.'

'I worked that out. Let's get back to the digging thing. I've never dug anything in my entire life.'

The man softly laughed. 'Is your baby due soon?'

'*Baby?*'

He reddened, and tried to stammer an apology.

'I'm kidding. It was due about a week ago.'

'Oh, thank god for that. I mean... you know.'

'Sorry. Couldn't resist a little joke.'

'Laughter is the best medicine, right?'

'So they say.'

'Listen, you don't know me from Adam, which is funny because my name is Adam. But I'm pleased to meet you.'

'I'm Jennifer.' She proffered her hand and he shook it. His grip was, as she had predicted, strong; but gentle. He was really a very nice man.

'My brother spent most of yesterday evening in tears.'

'Oh dear. Me too.'

'He is truly sorry.'

Jennifer thought for a moment. 'What happened? What did you see, exactly?'

'It was as your daughter said. There was another dog on the opposite side of the street, barking. Your dog barked back at it, and I saw your daughter struggle to hold him. Then he freed himself and ran out. But it all happened so quick. All at once. You know.'

'I see. What's your brother's name?'

'Rich. Richard.'

'Could you thank him for the flowers? And perhaps tell him that yellow flowers are my favourite. I love yellow.'

'That's... serendipitous. A great guess. All right. I'll pass that on. How is your daughter doing?'

'I've no idea. She hasn't come home yet.'

'Really? Where is she?'

'I don't know.' It was all too much. So much emotion in her life these days. Was it all falling apart, truly?

162

'Can I make you a cup of tea?' said Adam.

'Would you mind?'

Over tea, rather badly but kindly made, Jennifer told him, Adam, a stranger, everything. Her life story. She left nothing out: not her dreadful marriage to the despicable Patrick, not her promiscuity, not even her termination and the giving-up of Marnie as a baby. Not even Ethan's role in the pregnancy, not the loss of her best friend. Adam was easy to talk to. He listened, this stranger, without judgement. Perfect conditions for pouring out your heart, which Jennifer did.

'So there you have it. My life.'

'You have lived, Jennifer.'

'But it's been charmless.'

'But you are not without charm. I can assure you.'

If Jennifer was the blushing type, she would have been bright red at that point. But she wasn't, and she wasn't. 'Thank you,' she said.

'How about you ring Marnie? You need to know she's in one piece. Tell her to come home.'

'Do you think this is her home?'

'Don't you?'

'Yes. Yes, I think it probably is. Time will tell.'

Jennifer rubbed her belly.

'You OK?'

'Yes, I think so. Just a Braxton-Hicks.'

'A what?'

'It's a Braxton-Hicks contraction. Like a practice for the real thing.'

'You're sure it's not the real thing?'

'I'm sure. They've been strong for a few days now.'

Jennifer picked up her mobile and called Marnie's number. Adam waited patiently, looking around the kitchen.

'Straight to voice mail,' said Jennifer.

'Text her?'

'I will.'

'Listen, I've got to go. It was lovely to meet you properly and learn more about you. If you want to... let me leave you my number. I would love to take you to dinner sometime. In due course. When you're... less busy, shall we say?'

'I see. Less pregnant, you mean? Pop your number in my phone, could you, please?'

Jennifer watched Adam as he did so. He handed back the phone.

'Thanks.'

'Let's meet up when you're ready. *If* you're ready. No problem if it never happens.'

'Thank you for listening. And for your help yesterday. And please... pass on to your brother my... what's the right word...?'

'Forgiveness?'

'Sounds a bit lofty, but OK. Please let your brother know I don't hold it against him. It was one of those things. If anything it was my fault. Jake is... *was* a big dog and Marnie isn't used to dogs. I should have taken him out myself.'

'I'll talk to Rich. You talk to your daughter when she comes home.'

'I will. Don't worry.'

But Marnie didn't come home. Adam had finally taken his leave. He'd acted like he didn't want to go. He had kept looking anxiously at her bump, at her hand stroking her bump.

Of course, she had lied to him. These contractions were stronger than Braxton-Hicks. After waving Adam off, watching his sporty little car purr away, she closed the door, went upstairs, brought down her pre-packed hospital bag, and started timing the contractions. She consulted her pregnancy books. There was *probably* no need to panic. The contractions were regular but not very close together, yet. Eight or nine minutes.

She sent Marnie a text, after much deliberation: *I'm in labour, heading for the Princess Louise hospital soon. No panic. Contractions strong, regular, but not close yet. All is forgiven. That man who helped came back this morn. He brought us flowers from his bro. I know it wasn't your fault, or anybody else's. I'm sorry. Come home. Or go to the hospital. Love J x (Mum)*

How to get to the hospital? Should she drive herself? The contractions were... uncomfortable. Possibly they would render driving difficult; therefore, dangerous. But if she timed it right she might be able to get there between contractions. It was a sedate ten minute drive from her house.

Oh, *where* was Marnie? Why had she been so unkind, so cold towards the poor girl? Where did she get off behaving like that? Her daughter, a truly lovely young woman, returning to her, wanting to be in her life... *come back, Marnie. Come home.*

Jennifer fetched the baby seat from the dining room, and spent a few minutes figuring out how to strap it into the back seat of her car. Perhaps she should have put it in weeks ago, or at least practised. She had to pause halfway through her efforts for a contraction. It was strong, the strongest yet. Surely she was in labour. It didn't feel like a false alarm. She checked her watch. Seven and a half minutes since the start of the last one. She tried to recall her labour with Marnie. But it was vague, lost to her. All she could recall was the huge sense of relief after Marnie was born.

She went back into the house, and checked that all doors and windows were locked. She glanced at Jake's bowls on the floor in the kitchen. They still contained the remains of his water, his last meal. No time now. She would have to clear it all away when she got home. Whenever that would be. She left a note for Kimberley and Scott, both of whom would be turning up at nine o'clock tomorrow morning. Kimberley had a house key. They would find the note.

Excited, scared, she locked the front door, and eased herself into her car. Only Marnie knew where she was heading, and that's just how she wanted it. This was about family, and family only. Fleetingly, in her mind's eye, she saw an anxious Alison. *Oh, Jennifer...* and she banished the thought, she let it go. She started the car, and slowly pulled away, heading to the hospital and whatever might happen there.

Epidural

She didn't tell the midwives she had driven herself. She deliberately parked her car in the furthest reaches of the car park, under an old oak tree.

She was checked in, a few tests were ran, she was settled into a delivery room, and... nothing. The contractions slowed, became less painful. Was it a false alarm after all? She had, weeks ago, requested a water birth; and, mercifully, one of the two water birth delivery rooms was free. She wasn't really sure why she wanted a water birth. Mainly for the pain relief. She had a coward's heart, she knew. She wasn't happy-clappy, hippy-trippy. Far from it.

But it wasn't time to prepare the pool yet, said her midwife. *Oh?*

You have hours to go, said the busy thirty-something, and she bustled from the room to attend to another delivery. The sounds of screams and screeches reached Jennifer, and she shut the door. There was a digital radio on the high window sill, so she switched it on and tuned it from the crappy commercial local station to 6 Music.

Emptying out her bag and arranging things to her satisfaction took all of ten minutes, not even hampered by a weak contraction. God forbid she would be sent home again... the worst outcome, surely?

She sat in the chair alongside the bed and opened her book. She was reading a door-stopper: *A Woman of Substance* by Barbara Taylor Bradford. About a third in now, and she was thoroughly enjoying it. She liked Emma. She liked the woman she was becoming.

She read a page; realised she hadn't taken a word in; started again. She was hot. Could she open the window? She did so, and enjoyed the warm breeze that flooded in. She read again, concentrating this time, and finished a chapter and almost a second one when she realised the contractions were becoming stronger again. Frequent too. She had to breathe deeply. Time to get the midwife's attention? She had been on her own for an hour, maybe more, now. Surely it wasn't meant to be like this? Where was the fussing? The drama? She was thirsty. Was there a water cooler out in the corridor?

She stuck her head out of the door. Heard the wretched screams. Spotted the water cooler. Made for it. Then: a gush, everywhere, fluid, warm, splashing on to the floor. Jennifer looked down. Her sandals, feet, legs, were wet. On the floor, a puddle. So she wouldn't be sent home after all.

'Oh,' she said to herself. *Here comes the drama.* Then: 'Hello?!'

'OK?' said the midwife – Emma, funnily enough – as she looked at the monitor. The epidural was working. It was utter bliss after the three hours of labour she had endured with nothing but the pool for pain relief. Pain relief, her arse! She had started begging for the epidural after an hour in the pool. There was just one anaesthetist on duty, because it was a Sunday. She was already busy with another delivery. Jennifer would have to wait. The midwife bustled from the room to procure "a ball", which she came back with a few minutes later, suggesting Jennifer use that.

'May I ask,' said Jennifer through clenched teeth, 'how a... *space-hopper* is going to stop this god-awful pain? Are you out of your fucking mind, Emma?'

'It's not a... what did you call it?'

'A space-hopper. Never mind. You probably had to be there.'

'It's not a "space-hopper".'

'It bloody looks like one. Stick a slightly threatening smiley face on it and it's a dead ringer. Take it away, Emma. I want an epidural. Please. As soon as possible.'

Emma deposited the space hopper alongside the abandoned birthing pool. She checked Jennifer's cervix. Three-and-a-half centimetres. Which was both good and bad news. Bad because all the pain so far had only produced such a small dilation; good because it wasn't too late to have an epidural. Which Jennifer wanted. No question. *Now.*

'You're doing really well, Jenny,' said Emma.

'Jennifer.'

'Jennifer. Sorry.'

'I don't care if I'm doing well, or not. That's not the point. I want an epidural.'

'I'll go and see how the anaesthetist is getting on.'

'Thank you.' And another contraction started to build. Emma left the room and the contraction grew. *It hurts! So much. I'm all alone with this. But who can I call? Nobody. There's nobody. It's just me and my baby girl. And Emma. And a space-hopper.*

And then the bliss of the epidural, the contractions reduced to data on a monitor, which Emma carefully studied. The pain was there, hovering, Jennifer could feel it... but somehow the pain was screened-out, reduced to a notion, an absent idea...it felt rather surreal, but better than the alternative, quite enough of which she had experienced before the anaesthetist worked her magic. Sitting still for the needle had been the hardest part; Emma had held her hands, talked her softly through it. A consultant obstetrician had then swanned in, looked at Jennifer's notes, patronised Emma, patronised Jennifer, and swanned out again, apparently satisfied that all was well. He had on a white suit, and the heels on his shiny shoes went clickety-clack.

'You were honoured,' said Emma.

'It's my age, isn't it? I'm a geriatric, obstetrically-speaking.'

'I think that was the reason he visited, yes. I'm surprised he was around on a Sunday.'

'Is everything OK?'

'Yes, I think so. The baby's heart beat is regular, your stats are all great. The contractions have slowed and weakened a little, but that's normal after an epidural.'

'How much longer do you think it will be?'

'Until lift off? Hard to say. The contractions should come back up. I'll check your dilation again soon. Is there... somebody... do you have a birth partner?'

'No. I don't. I was hoping my grown-up daughter would make it, but she's... she must be busy. I fell out with my best friend. Otherwise I would have asked her to be my doula. Is that the word?'

'Yes, if you like, a doula. That's a pity. Why did you fall out, then?'

'Because her son is the father of this baby.'

'Oh. But that's... rather nice, isn't it?'

'It would be, but he's only eighteen. Actually I think he will soon be nineteen.'

Emma, who surely must have seen and heard it all by now, coughed. But her face betrayed nothing. She was a professional.

'I'll check your cervix again.'

170

*

Two hours into the beautiful epidural, the monitor was displaying the increasing intensity of the contractions. Jennifer realised she had perhaps lived her whole life with an epidural. Anaesthetised. Cut off... from what? Love? Family? Friends? Work? She had never done a day of paid employment. What was she so scared of? Pain. Of course, she was scared of pain. Like most people, she tried to avoid it. Perhaps that was cowardly. *No coward heart is mine...* who wrote that? It had suddenly come to her. From her school days. Was it a Bronte poem?

But this self-analysis would all have to come later. For now, she had a baby to give birth to.

'OK, Jennifer, it's time to start pushing,' announced Emma. 'Are you in?'

Jennifer smiled. 'I'm in.'

And the delivery room door was shoved open, with a bang, and there was Marnie, hot-looking, dusty-looking, dishevelled, red-faced. 'Mum!'

'Oh! You made it! I have to start pushing now. This is my midwife, Emma. Emma, this is my daughter, Marnie.'

Emma looked delighted; relieved, even. 'What a beautiful name.'

'I chose it,' said Jennifer.

'Shall I hold your hand?' said Marnie.

'Wait,' said Emma, noticing Marnie's bump. 'Are you a mum-to-be too?'

'Yep!'

'How lovely.'

'Yes, Marnie, please do hold my hand!' said Jennifer.

'My sister is gonna be born on my birthday,' said Marnie.

'I'd forgotten!' cried Jennifer.

'How lovely,' said Emma.

'Don't worry, Mum. My birthday isn't important. Just get my sister out safely.'

'I'm trying.'

And twenty minutes later, Emma said the head was out. 'Pant now, Jennifer, pant!' ordered Emma. This was the first time she had shown even a hint of urgency. She really was a perfect midwife – calm, and compassionate, measured, kind, but authoritative.

'Oh, Mum! I can see her face!'

'And here she comes...' said Emma.

Jennifer looked down, saw a grey-ish, blue-ish, cottage-cheese-covered being, and saw Marnie crying, and Emma busy. The being was lifted up to Jennifer, covered in a sheet, and the being, a baby, a human, started to cry too. So Jennifer did the only decent thing, and she cried as well, kissing her new daughter's head, the drug-like deliciousness of her baby's smell just the first of the many thrills she knew this new life was going to bring her.

The Phone Call III

Alison looked up from her cross stitch. Ethan's mobile was ringing. Ethan was in the kitchen. Alison leaned across the sofa and picked up the phone. "Marnie". Who was that? Perhaps Ethan's mystery girl? A new girl?

'It's Marnie!' Alison called. The phone stopped ringing. Ethan came through into the lounge with three glasses of lemonade. 'I'll call her back,' said Ethan. 'Where's Dad?'

'In the loo. Reading. Who's this Marnie, then?'

'Dad! Cold drink!'

Alison took hers. The ice cubes chinked in the glass. It was so hot again... every day was hot. But they were all getting used to it.

Ethan picked up his phone and Malcolm sauntered into the lounge. He took up his glass.

'All right, Marnie?' said Ethan. 'OK... OK... that's good news, then... yes. Can I come over today? OK... sure... I'll head over now. Thanks.'

Alison and Malcolm paused their drinking and waited. Ethan stared into the distance, if there was any distance in their rather small – but comfortable – lounge.

'Well?' said Alison eventually.

'Jennifer's had the baby.'

'So... who is Marnie?' Alison said.

'I'm going to the hospital,' Ethan said.

Malcolm leaped up. 'I'll drive you, son.'

'It'll only be for a few minutes.'

'I'll drive you.'

'Thanks, Dad.'

They both looked at Alison. Nothing. They looked at each other. Shrugged.

'Let's go,' said Malcolm.

'Who is Marnie?!' Alison called after them.

She heard the car roar off... well, a Malcolm-style roar-off, which was a slightly pacier acceleration than normal. He was the most sedate of drivers. Boring, some would say. *Safe.* She preferred the word safe. She finished her lemonade. They had wanted her to go with them. Should she have done? Of course not. That would be some kind of tacit approval of this whole sordid situation. This... circus. Her teenage son, barely out of nappies himself, a father. Jennifer, old enough to be his mother. Older than *her*, his actual mother. How it went round and round in her head, how it tortured her. And Malcolm, so... what was the word... accepting? Yes, accepting! Of this awful situation. Her son's life, ruined... Malcolm had said, only the other evening, "Not ruined, Alison. *Changed.* Jennifer is being very reasonable about it." *Reasonable?!* Seducing her own nephew? As good as, anyway. OK, not really a nephew in a biological sense. But a nephew in all other ways.

Who was Marnie?

She was missing something.

She was missing Jennifer. That was the truth. Strip away the anger, the dismay, the torturous thoughts, the *Victorian levels of disapproval*, as Ethan had muttered recently... and what was left was the simple shining truth that she missed her friend. The closest thing she'd ever had to a sister. Gone, just like that, and this time for ever. There was no coming back from this, no forgiveness. Not this time.

This Marnie must be a new friend of Jennifer's. Perhaps they had met at an antenatal class, or something. But hadn't Ethan said Jennifer had opted not to attend any classes? So who was she? It wasn't her business, she had to remind herself. Not her business at all.

Visitors

'Hello?'

It was Malcolm. At least, it sounded like him. He was hidden by the biggest bunch of flowers she had ever seen. Carnations, gerbera, roses. A multitude of colours. 'Come on in, Malcolm.'

She had her own room, of course. Paid for. Booked in advance. Baby Sawyer was snuggled in the Perspex cot alongside the bed. Her little woollen hat was like a doll's hat. She was so small. Seven pounds exactly, so not *that* small... but small, and perfect, and red, and pale, all at the same time. Human and not-human at the same time. Ethereal, Jennifer supposed. Marnie had already had her cuddle, welcoming her baby half-sister into this "big bad world".

'Didn't the midwives tell you flowers aren't allowed, Malc?' Jennifer said, not unkindly.

'They did. They also said I could show them to you. I can drop them around to yours after we've left, if you like?'

'Would you? We should be home tomorrow. Marnie, give Malc your key, would you?'

'Where's Ethan?' said Marnie, rooting around in her bag.

'He's... outside,' said Malcolm. 'He had to sit down for a moment to collect his thoughts. Something like that.'

'Ah,' said Jennifer.

'Shall I send him in? Marnie and I can give you space.'

Marnie handed the key to Malcolm. 'Sure we can,' she said.

'I'll pop the flowers back to the car,' said Malcolm.

'Thanks, Malc. Come and have a good look at your granddaughter first, though?'

'Of course.' Malcolm approached the bed. 'But even before that, a hug,' he said. 'You clever old thing!' He leaned towards Jennifer and held out his arms. He was crying, but in a very understated, Malcolm-like way. He hugged her.

'Oh, Malc. You're so kind. Isn't she gorgeous?'

Malcolm smiled his biggest smile, peered into the cot, and wiped his tears. 'She is. I wouldn't have expected anything less.'

'Perhaps have a cuddle later, eh?' said Jennifer. Malcolm nodded.

Then he and Marnie shuffled from the room. Jennifer sat up in bed, wincing, and she smoothed her hair. She knew she didn't look her best. No make-up, and she was beyond tired; emotionally she felt like a Catherine wheel. But none of that mattered.

Ethan slowly pushed open the door. 'Can I come in?' he said.

'Yes. Ethan, come in. I think you should, don't you?'

He entered, and closed the door behind him.

'It's a girl, then?' he said. 'The scan was right?'

'Yes. You have a daughter.'

Ethan looked stricken. Shocked. Terrified.

'Would you like to hold her?'

'Isn't she asleep?'

'Yes. Come and have a look at her, at least.'

Ethan approached the cot. He leaned over, stared, bit his lip. His eyes wide. 'Oh my God. She's beautiful.'

Jennifer beamed at him. 'She is.'

'I can't believe... I can't believe I am a father. *Her* father.'

'It's a lot to take in, isn't it? If it helps I've been having similar feelings. I wasn't expecting this at my age, you know? And neither were you.'

'No.'

'It will be all right. We'll sort it all out. Like I said, for now I'm content to be a single parent. I'm quite realistic about that. Your time will come, Ethan.'

'Thank you.'

'I've chosen her name. I wanted to tell you first.'

'OK.'

'Emma Rose... Sawyer.'

Ethan said nothing for a few moments. Then: 'Emma is a pretty name. And Rose. They suit her.'

'Thank you, Ethan.'

'Mum wouldn't come with us.'

'I gathered that.'

'She's being pathetic, actually.'

'Maybe. A little. But it's hard for her. You're *her* baby, you see.'

'Will you add my name to the birth certificate?'

Silence.

Ethan stood over the cot of his daughter. 'I want her to know who I am.'

'She'll know! Don't worry about that.'

'She needs a dad. And grandparents.'

'It looks like she'll have a granddad. Malc was in bits for a minute! Smitten, I'd say.'

'He's a good guy, my dad. The best.'

'I know. You're a lucky lad, Ethan Timmins. You've got great parents.'

'Knock, knock...?' Malcolm slowly pushed open the door. He and Marnie came back in. Then a midwife poked her head round the door.

178

'That's it for visiting now, I'm afraid,' she said.

'Righto,' said Malcolm.

'Before you go,' said Jennifer, 'Ethan has something to tell you both.'

'Do I?'

'Your daughter's name...?'

'Oh! Sure. She's gonna be called Emma Rose.'

'Very pretty,' said Malcolm.

Marnie grimaced. Jennifer ignored her.

'Emma Rose Sawyer,' continued Malcolm. 'That has a lovely ring to it.'

Jennifer looked at Ethan. He looked at her.

'Emma Rose Sawyer-*Timmins*,' said Jennifer.

'Even better,' said Malcolm. 'Bit of a mouthful... but it makes sense.'

'It makes perfect sense,' said Jennifer. And then it was Ethan's turn to wipe away the tears.

After the menfolk had left, Emma Rose Sawyer-Timmins woke up, demanding to be fed. Marnie lifted the squalling baby from the cot and passed her to her mother. Jennifer fed Emma Rose. It seemed... easy. Not something she had planned on doing beyond the colostrum of the early days... but now... well, now she thought she might carry on with it.

'I'd better go,' said Marnie.

'No! I mean, no, please don't. Stay. They can put one of those fold-out beds in here for you.'

'They won't like that.'

'I'm paying. They don't have to like it. I want the three of us to be together this night. Her first on earth. Well, outside of my body.' Jennifer felt her face crumple.

'Mum?' Marnie sat alongside Jennifer and Emma Rose. She put her arm round Jennifer's shoulders. 'It's all good.'

'I know!' sobbed Jennifer. 'That's what I'm frightened of!'

'Good things aren't to be feared.'

'And then you have to go through this too. Soon. So soon!'

'I'll be fine, Mum. Calm down. OK?'

'I'm sorry. I'm all over the place right now. I know you'll be fine. They're great here. Really they are.'

'Oh, I'm not having my baby in hospital. I've changed my mind. I'm having a home birth.'

Sore

Jennifer's house was a mess; and so was she. Baby Emma had jaws like clamps, and breastfeeding, so easy at first, so joyful, so euphoric, had become agonising. Jennifer's milk had come in, so her breasts were sore and full, bloated. Jennifer sent Marnie out to Boots for calendula cream and a breast pump. The midwife's idea. "Try something else, *my lovely*," she said. Which sounded odd as the midwife was about twenty-eight and had tattoos and a nose piercing, which Marnie admired. The midwife tried to help Jennifer with positioning. In the end Jennifer had to ask her to stop. She had been prodded and midwife-handled once too often.

The breast pump would be more gentle, the midwife reassured Jennifer. Things would heal and then she could continue breast-feeding. If she wanted to. Marnie helped with washing and sterilising the bottles. They had an argument over the reusable nappies versus the Pampers. Pampers won.

'For now!' said Marnie.

'Whatever,' said Jennifer.

The funky midwife, Willow (apparently), was all for Marnie having a home birth.

'What if something goes wrong?' asked Jennifer.

'I'll monitor the baby and if I think something is "going wrong", we'll get to the Princess Louise. I'll let them know you're in labour, Marnie, so they'll be sort-of on standby. Another midwife will be here too for the actual birth.'

'That sounds OK,' said Jennifer. Her phone pinged. Could it be Alison?!

Hey, it's Adam. Hope ur doing OK. Call me when ur ready. Rich was relieved to get ur forgiveness. He's doing OK now. Driving again. Hope we can have that dinner sometime. Take care.

She had not heard from Alison. Nothing at all. Not a text, not a call, not a card. Ethan and Malcolm had visited yesterday, bringing another bunch of flowers (still not yellow, but Jennifer liked other colours too, so it mattered not) and a bottle of very nice Prosecco, which Malcolm took great pride in uncorking and pouring. Jennifer took tiny sips from her glass. She wasn't sure if she still liked alcohol, or should be drinking it while breast-feeding.

Jennifer texted Adam back. It was only fair. And somewhere at the back of her mind, at the back of her life, this new amazing and crazy life, she knew she was attracted to him. She liked him. He seemed like a very nice man. Perhaps the circumstances of their meeting had been less than ideal. Tragic, even. But that wasn't his fault or hers. *I'm fine, thanks. Had the baby at the weekend. A girl named Emma Rose. Healthy and greedy! I'll get back to you about that dinner once life is not quite so upside down.*

Seconds later: *Congratulations. Wonderful news. So glad for you. See you when you are ready, I hope. I'll wait, happy to.*

Later, after Willow had gone to see other new mums, and Marnie was hanging out two large loads of laundry, Jennifer tried the breast pump. Marnie has sterilised it, and Willow had set it up for her. It felt odd, but it was more gentle than Emma's greedy little mouth. Very little milk seemed to come out. No wonder Emma was so hungry all the time.

Emma started to cry for feeding just as Jennifer felt she had drained both sides. Perfect. At first the stubborn little baby twisted and turned away from the bottle. Then she seemed to understand what was in it, and she sucked greedily and quickly. Once Emma had drained the bottle, Jennifer held her upright and wandered around the kitchen-diner. Emma wasn't great at burping, and it took time. Jennifer still expected Jake to get up from his bed by the patio doors and trot over to her. His food and drink bowls had gone, Jennifer noticed. Marnie must have cleared them. His bed was still there though. Perhaps she could ask Malcolm to take it to the dump for her? It was tatty and stained and a bit chewed, and nobody else would want it.

'She took the bottle,' Jennifer said when Marnie came back in with the now-empty washing baskets. Jennifer jigged her baby up and down, back and forth.

'Cool,' said Marnie, and she returned to the kitchen's laundry end and sorted washing into piles. They had got rather behind with it. Emma was getting through onesies at an alarming rate. 'I'll get another load on. It should all dry. It would be a shame to waste all this drying weather. Listen to me! I sound like a washing powder advert.'

Jennifer burst into tears. Yet again. Marnie got up and went to her, putting her arm around her free shoulder. 'Mum...?'

'It's all right. I'm sorry. It's the baby blues, I think. All the books said this would happen.'

'Oh god. I've all this to look forward to.'

'We'll be crying into our coffees together.'

'Is it just the baby blues?'

Jennifer paused, sniffed. 'No. Probably not.'

'Is it Alison?'

'Yes.'

'You've still not heard from her?'

'No.'

'That's a shame, Mum.'

'Yes. I wanted to ask her advice, you know?'

'She'll come round, won't she? I mean she'll get in touch in the end. And come round. Surely she'll want to meet her granddaughter?'

'You'd think so, wouldn't you? But she has this streak in her... sort of unforgiving and hard. But she's normally such a soft person. It's difficult to explain. Puritanical, almost. Over-protective of Ethan, too.'

'I understand. My foster mother was a bit like that.'

'I'm sorry.'

'What for?'

'Not keeping you. Being selfish.'

'Mum, we've been over this, haven't we? It wasn't great, but neither was it awful. OK?'

Jennifer smiled at her. 'Thank you. Just look at me. Two beautiful daughters, a beautiful home that's mine-all-mine, a great little car, a gardener... a great life, you know? I've nothing to complain about.'

'But you'd trade the house and the car to have your old friend back in your life. Am I right?'

'Yes, Marnie, you're right.'

'I'm sorry, Mum. There's still hope, isn't there? In the meantime you've got to look after yourself. You look knackered. Let me take Emma for a while and you go for a nap.'

'Thank you. What would I do without you?'

'Dunno. I'll clean up too.'

'Don't go too mad. Kimberley is popping in tomorrow to do a general once over. Perhaps just tidy up a bit? But she'll do the rest.'

Jennifer went to bed and slept for an hour. Then she woke to her baby's cries, and Marnie bringing her into the bedroom.

'I've not time to pump any milk off. I'll have to feed her myself,' said Jennifer.

'We just need to get into a routine. That's all. I've washed the pump again and stuck it in the chlorine bucket.'

'Thank you. What a life! It's so alien yet so... natural? Is that the word?'

'Probably. Ethan rang me. He's asked me to go for a drink with him to celebrate Emma and to get to know me better. He says.'

'Are you going to go?'

'Yeah. Tomorrow. He feels a bit like a brother, you know? A little brother.'

'Yes, I suppose he must do. You should go. Have a nice meal or something.'

Visitors II

Alison turned off the hoover and went to the front door. She had only just heard it ring.

'Helena.'

Helena entered. She didn't even say hello. Alison followed her into the lounge. 'I'm afraid I don't have homemade biscuits today,' said Alison. 'I wasn't expecting you.'

'Sorry not sorry.'

'OK.'

Helena sat down heavily on the sofa, scowling, arms crossed.

'What's the matter, then?' said Alison. *Dear oh dear... this girl could be rather demanding when she wanted to be.*

'It's Ethan. I think he has a new girlfriend.'

'Oh? What makes you think that?'

'I saw him out on Friday night. He was in Pizza Express.'

'And?'

'He was with a girl.'

'Ah. I mean... Oh.'

'She was fat.'

Alison ignored the remark. *Pot, kettle, and black.*

'Perhaps she is just a friend,' said Alison. Ethan had gone out on Friday night, but Alison hadn't asked where or who with. She wasn't her son's keeper.

'Perhaps not.'

'I'll make us coffee.'

'Tea for me.'

Alison made the drinks. She found a few shop-bought biscuits left at the bottom of the barrel. She was due to order her online groceries today. She had planned to do that after hoovering.

'Helena, did you know that Ethan's... the baby was born, last week?'

'No. Why would I know?'

'It's a little girl, apparently. She's doing fine, Malcolm tells me.'

'God almighty. Poor little thing. An old slapper for a mother and a philandering bastard for a father.'

'Oh, come on, Helena.'

'It's true, isn't it?'

'Jennifer is certainly a fan of men.'

'Ethan is a bastard. Like this poor little baby. Like father like daughter.'

'Try not to be bitter, love.'

'Can't help it.'

Helena ate a biscuit, crumbs scattering all over the sofa and the carpet. She didn't seem to notice. *Try not to be bitter, love.* Malcolm had spoken those very words to Alison only yesterday. He'd suggested, quietly, again, that she should meet her granddaughter. Alison has rebuffed the idea. *No. No, Malcolm. And stop bringing it up.*

Helena stayed for an hour, and slagged Ethan off the whole time, until in the end Alison felt she had to get a bit firmer with her.

'He is my son, Helena. And he's made a dreadful mistake. But he's not evil. All right?'

187

Helena looked at her through narrowed eyes. Alison felt scrutinised. So she stood up, made an excuse. She had to get on. She had a dentist appointment at... one. She didn't want to be late.

The doorbell rang just as they entered the hallway. Alison squeezed past Helena and opened the door.

'Are you Alison?' said the young woman standing before her. She was rather pretty, if hippy-ish. Strange hair. Striking hair.

'Yes.'

'It's her!' cried Helena, pushing Alison to one side.

'Who?' said Alison, cross now. Really, Helena could be unbearably rude.

'Who the hell are you?' said the young woman.

'I'm Ethan's girlfriend.'

'Well,' said Alison, her composure – if she ever really had any – recovered. 'You're not. You're his former girlfriend.'

'Are you Helena?' said this hippy-ish young woman.

'Yeah. That's right.'

'Ethan's ex?'

Helena winced. 'I suppose so, now.'

'He told me all about you.'

Silence. Helena looked the girl up and down. Her eyes lingered on her belly, and Alison's did too.

'Are you pregnant?' asked Helena.

'Well spotted, Miss Marple.'

'And don't tell me, it's Ethan's?'

Alison cried out, or gasped, or something.

The young woman put out a steadying hand to her. 'Are you all right?'

'I don't know. Who are you?'

'I'm Marnie. Jennifer's daughter.'

'Her *what*?' cried Alison.

'This just gets better and better,' said Helena.

Marnie II

Helena pushed past Marnie, smirking. Her eyes lingered on the tattoo. So did Alison's. Marnie was wearing a pair of denim cut-offs (which, Alison surmised, she had let out herself, judging by the resourceful use of safety pins and shoe laces). She wore a white shirt. Her hair was all sort-of coiled up on her head, loosely, and looked like it would tumble down at any moment. But Alison had the feeling it wouldn't. On her feet were an old pair of blue Converse, worn and tatty. She was stylish, in her own way. But Jennifer's *daughter*? No! It couldn't be right. Alison examined the girl's face. There was a resemblance. This girl was extremely pretty. Of course. She wondered who the father might have been... and she couldn't even frame the thought that Jennifer had a grown-up daughter; and had never said, never let on, never revealed this momentous thing.

Helena left, leaving Alison and Marnie standing awkwardly in the doorway.

'I didn't know Jennifer had another child,' said Alison.

'Yeah, she did. It's me!' said Marnie.

What else didn't Alison know about Jennifer? Her friend. Her longest-standing friend. The friend who had rescued her at school on that very first day. Something to be grateful for. But did she even know her? Had she ever known her? Had it ever really been a friendship? When had she given birth to this child?

'How old are you?'

'Just turned twenty-four.'

Alison did some mental maths. Never her strong point. Twenty-four years ago... 'You were born in nineteen... ninety-four?'

'Yeah.'

'I see.' That was during one of their breaks. Jennifer going her own way, all those lovers of hers, then Patrick... Alison and Malcolm planning their wedding. But they had been in touch, still, during that era. Birthday cards, usually with catch-up notes. But Jennifer didn't tell her about having a baby. Why...? What...? 'Would you like to come in for a nice cold drink?'

'Yeah. Thanks.'

Marnie sunk into the sofa and stretched out her long legs. The tattoo was remarkable, and undeniably attractive. Alison didn't generally approve of tattoos. Thank God, Malcolm had never got one. She didn't think Ethan had either.

Alison brought them both a glass of her homemade lemonade, ice cubes popping and clicking, melting rapidly in the endless heat. Marnie drank hers swiftly.

'Another?' said Alison.

'Maybe in a bit. Really nice drink, that.'

'I can give you the recipe.'

'Sure thing.'

Alison sipped her own lemonade and wondered what to say. Where to start. There were a lot of questions. 'Jennifer never told me about you,' she said in the end.

'Yeah, I know. She didn't tell anyone.'

'Do you know who your father is?'

'Nope.'

'I see.'

'I was put up for adoption. But I was never adopted. I had a long term foster family and I fell out with them, then my foster mum died. Then I got pregnant by a fifty-two year old—' Alison almost spat out her lemonade but managed to swallow it instead '—and I got kicked out of where I was living. That's when I decided to find my real mum.'

'Was that easy to do?

'Yes. The Internet pretty much makes nobody invisible these days.'

'That's true. Did... did Jennifer choose your name?'

'Yes.'

'It's a very stylish name.'

'My sister is Emma Rose.'

'Yes. Ethan mentioned that to me.'

'It's a pretty name too.'

'Yes.'

'My mum has good taste. You know she lost her dog? It was my fault. I couldn't hold him on his lead and he got ran over. It caused a big fall out.'

'I heard, yes. That's rather sad. Jennifer set a lot of store by that dog.'

'I thought she would never speak to me again. I ran away. Stayed over night in the park.'

'My goodness.'

'It's so hot at the moment so I didn't get cold.'

'You know he was really called Samson?' said Alison, suddenly recalling this fact. 'But she insisted he was Jake. To spite her husband.'

'Oh yeah. The one who beat her up.'

Alison felt her face go pale. She put down her glass. 'Patrick?'

'Yep. Nasty piece of work. Didn't you know?'

'He was rather controlling. But we didn't really know him.'

'Just as well. Bullying bastard. Mum set Jake on him in the end. That dog was a bloody hero.'

'Evidently.'

'So I was quite surprised when Jennifer – Mum – forgave me. But she did. And now we get along just fine.'

'Yes. I'm pleased for you, Marie.'

'Marnie.'

'Forgive me. Marnie. Look, I know what you are try—'

'So don't you think you could forgive her like she forgave me?'

'It's complicated.'

'Not really. You have a granddaughter. She's all that matters. And she's gorgeous.'

'Marnie—'

'I came round here to say hello to my baby sister's grandmother and also to see if I can persuade you to make it up with my mum.'

'I realise that.'

'But it's not going to happen?'

'No.'

'Why not?'

'The entire situation is obscene.'

'It's not!'

'You're young. You don't understand. You've never—'

'Yes, I'm young, but I've been through a lot in my life and it wasn't great and do you know what? I have forgiveness in my heart. So does Jennifer. She forgave me for not looking after Jake. I forgave her for giving me up for the adoption-that-never-happened. What's your problem with forgiveness? It's fucking easy.'

'Please don't swear.'

Marnie giggled.

'What's funny?'

'Mum warned me about your puritanical streak.'

'And did she send you on this little mission?'

'No! She'd go mental if she knew. I just decided to come round and see if I can talk some sense into you.'

Alison stood. 'I need to get on.'

Marnie stared at her for a few moments. Then she stood too. She left the lounge and made for the front door, Alison following. Marnie couldn't open the door so Alison did it for her.

'It's a bit awkward,' Alison mumbled.

'You can say that again,' said Marnie as she stepped out of the door. She turned to Alison. 'Nobody can make you change your mind or be part of Emma's life. But I know there is nothing more important than family, and like it or not, that's what this is all about. This is what we are. You, Malc, Ethan, Jennifer, Emma, me, my baby. We're family. It's the best thing in the world. My mum was your best friend once. Now she's related to you. How amazing is that?'

Alison smiled weakly. She had not really thought about it in these simple terms. 'It was nice to meet you, Marnie. But I'm afraid your rather cosy view of things isn't shared by me. It never will be. It can't be. It's all based on betrayal and... inappropriate behaviour.'

'Whatever. People aren't perfect, you know. People are "inappropriate". It's called human nature. Gotta go. Seeing my midwife at midday.'

Alison watched Marnie leave. Then she closed the door, retrieved the lemonade glasses from the lounge and took them to the kitchen to rinse out. She wondered again if she had ever really known Jennifer at all. All those years... And could it be true about Patrick? There had been something rather too studied about him, as if he was trying too hard to project a personality. A false one, Alison had suspected. But why hadn't Jennifer confided in her? About Patrick? About Marnie? She had a daughter?! Jennifer would have been... (more mental maths)... twenty-five? Twenty-six? *I just can't believe it.* Jennifer? A mother all those years, denying it completely. So anti-mother, almost. Anti-child. "Sprog", she had called Ethan, when he was little. Horrible disrespectful word. Acting like Ethan was a totally new experience... holding him at arm's length, literally. Alison recalled telling Jennifer all about Ethan's difficult birth and Jennifer had said nothing about her own experience... had feigned shock and surprise, even disgust. How could she do that? Live that kind of lie?

Then Alison thought of Danny Boy. That wild night of lust. That huge fat lie at the heart of her life, her marriage; long-buried but nevertheless real, lived, and denied. Regrettable. Wasn't it? *People aren't perfect, you know. People are "inappropriate".* Wise words, perhaps. That night had been inappropriate.

Alison turned off these thoughts. It was high time she got on with her supermarket shop. They were running out of milk. And biscuits. She didn't know anything anymore.

The Row

Alison flung back the duvet. She was getting so hot these days, suddenly and uncomfortably. The Change, as her mother had always called it; aloof and embarrassed when discussing – rarely – such things. Alison was in her late forties. It was that time in life. She had noticed her periods were becoming shorter and irregular; the last one had been a couple of weeks late. And that was six weeks ago or more. Had they stopped, and for ever? That wouldn't be so terrible. The good side of The Change, she supposed.

What would her mother say to her now, if she could? It was hard to imagine. Her mother had always held conflicting views. She had never quite approved of Jennifer. Yet she had never been unkind to her or about her. In fact they had got on rather well. Alison recalled, suddenly, her mother's funeral, and Jennifer's kind words, spoken quietly as she'd held Alison's trembling, cold hands in her own. She had bought the most beautiful flowers.

She listened to Malcolm as he showered. He was humming to himself. What a happy man he was. She envied him that; but also resented it. He seemed so excited to be a grandfather. He didn't share her disgust. Too philosophical, was Malcolm, too... forgiving? Was that even possible? To be *too* forgiving? Yes. Yes, it was. Despite Marnie's assertion that it was easy. It might be easy, but it was also called being a doormat. She was nobody's doormat.

Last night, she had held her tongue about Marnie's visit. In truth, she didn't know how to broach the subject. Did Malcolm know who she was? Did Ethan? She supposed they must know. Ethan has taken her to Pizza Express. In a way, Alison didn't want to know if they knew, or not. She didn't like, couldn't bear in fact, the idea of Malcolm and Ethan learning about the existence of Jennifer's older daughter before she did. It was disconcerting. Dismaying. What was the precise feeling? Horrible. Jealousy, she thought. Akin to jealousy. FOMO? That's the term Ethan might use.

The shower was turned off and after a couple of minutes Malcolm emerged from their tiny cramped en suite. He had wrapped his towel around his waist. He had always been a modest man. She tried not to notice his tiny paunch. He wasn't fat, not yet. She doubted he ever would be fat. But he was... getting looser. So was she, she supposed. Spreading, a bit. A lot. Now a size 16. Cellulite mushrooming in ever-new places. Such was life, she supposed. Everything changed, didn't it? She felt a certain amount of acceptance of her own body. She thought that was healthy. She had never been vain, unlike Jennifer.

Malcolm sprayed deodorant under his arm pits. Then he dropped the towel in order to get dressed. Alison looked away, making a pretence of checking her phone. She was modest too. Always had been. Never fully comfortable to be naked with her husband. It always made her feel defenceless. Not that she had ever needed to defend herself against Malcolm. He was not, never had been, never would be, that sort of man. He was not a Patrick. She has been thinking a lot about Patrick. Had he really beaten Jennifer up? Another thing kept from her. Why?

'I had a visitor yesterday,' she said, putting down her phone and looking at Malcolm once he had his underpants on. Navy blue boxers. Very Malcolm.

'Not that awful girl again.'

'Helena? What's so awful about her?'

'Come on, Alison...'

'I like her, in a way. I feel sorry for her. But no, not her. Well, yes, her... but then another girl came calling. Perhaps she's awful too? I don't know. Marnie.'

'Marnie came here?' He slowly buttoned his shirt.

'Yes.'

'What for?'

'I'm not sure.'

'Oh. Right. Nice girl, isn't she?'

'Tattoos aside, yes, she's fine. Nothing much like her mother.'

'She told you? Bit of a shock, all that, wasn't it?'

'Did you know?'

'Know what?'

'Malcolm...'

'Yes, I knew. Jennifer introduced her to us.'

'So Ethan knows too, who Marnie is?'

'Yes.'

'I can't believe Jennifer never told me about... it. Having a baby. Marnie. Whatever her name is.'

'Marnie. You got it right. Jennifer asked us to say nothing to you about her. I rather think she wanted to tell you herself.'

'So why didn't she tell me?'

Malcolm fell silent, fiddling with his shirt sleeve buttons. He was quite a smart dresser, in his own way. But not suave. He didn't quite pull off a suit like some men could. But he tried.

'Marnie's tattoos are rather off-putting,' Alison said.

'She's young.'

'And?'

'She's cool.'

'Is she.'

'I shouldn't be surprised if Ethan got one, you know. He mentioned that he might have Emma's name on his back. A bit Beckham-like.'

'God forbid. And, Malcolm?'

He was about to leave the bedroom to go downstairs for breakfast. Toast and tea, always. 'Yes?'

'I'd prefer it if... if you didn't mention any of this to me anymore. Jennifer and the baby and Marnie. I don't want to hear about any of it. As far as I'm concerned, they don't exist.'

Malcolm stopped in the doorway. He sighed. His shoulders slumped. Then he turned back towards her. He looked... angry. No. Cross. Cross was as angry as Malcolm ever got. 'You would deny your own granddaughter's existence?' His voice was cold, formal. He didn't speak like this. Except he just had.

'If you like. Yes.'

'I don't "like" it, Alison. How can you be so... so very horrible?'

'Horrible?'

'Yes. Mean. Cruel, even. Snobbish. Your mother making her presence f—'

'My mother?'

'She was a snooty cow.'

'How dare—?'

'No, you listen to me. I've had enough of this. Your mother was rotten when she wanted to be. Victorian. And until now, you haven't been. Try to keep it that way. What's done is done. Ethan and Jennifer have had a baby, and she's our granddaughter, and she might be the only grandchild we ever have. And she's... she's lovely. She's innocent.'

'I'm well aware of that.'

'And Jennifer is doing a great job and Ethan is coping and...

they could both use you. As a friend, as an experienced mother.'

'I think that's what Marnie was getting at. Jennifer sent her, I expect.'

'I doubt that. Marnie is a nice girl. Spirited. She desperately wants a family.'

'She has one. But I'm not in it.'

'Yes, you are. Whether you like it or not.'

'To quote you, I don't like it. I can't keep saying it, Malcolm.'

'In that case, don't.'

'Don't what?'

'Keep saying it. To be truthful, I'm sick of hearing it.'

'You're sick of it? I'm sick of it! Jennifer this, Emma that, Marnie, oh so perfect Marnie—'

'Are you jealous?'

'What?'

'Are you jealous?'

'Of what?'

'Jennifer has two kids. Two beautiful daughters. I know you wanted a daughter. She's wealthy, more than comfortable. She's a fine-looking woman. Glamorous. Her house is virtually a mansion. So are you jealous? Living in this cramped dusty little semi all these years with a teenage son you barely know anymore and a dud for a husband. Well? Is that it?'

'I—'

'Just say it. I can take it. I've always been boring. Right?'

'Malcolm! No. I love you, I love Ethan.'

'That doesn't mean I'm not boring.'

'Jennifer may hold that opinion of you. I don't.'

'I think she used to. We get on rather well now.'

'Bully for you!'

'Listen to yourself! You're a brat, Alison. A petulant brat.'

'I've never not loved you!'

'Sometimes it takes more than that.'

'What do you mean?'

'Acceptance. Of people, of situations.'

'I accept what's happened—'

'No, you don't. If you accepted it you'd be part of it.'

'Sounds like you're all getting on just fine without me!'

'Possibly we are. Who needs a sourpuss around?'

'Sourpuss?'

'Sorry.'

'Save it, Malcolm!'

'Don't come all holier than thou. I've had my fill of that.'

'Poor old Malcolm.'

'We can all surprise each other, at times.'

'Yes, I suppose so. But you've never surprised me, Malcolm. Not once. Not really. In all these years.'

'You want surprises? Shall we start now?'

'Why not?'

'I don't enjoy The Carpenters. I can't stand them. I'm more into AC/DC. And I hate that aftershave you buy me every Christmas. I never liked it, and I don't know where you got the idea from that I ever did. I don't like aftershave at all. I keep it hanging around for six months then I throw it away. I'm surprised you never noticed, to be honest.'

After a few seconds of silence, Alison asked, 'Anything else?' She thought she saw a look of (regretful?) triumph stalk across Malcolm's face. Haughty, almost, which was not like him. But he looked her straight in the eye, and he didn't flinch. An emotion like fear took hold of her.

'I know all about Danny Boy.'

Scarlett

'Mum?'

Jennifer rolled over in her bed to face her bedroom door. Beside her, Emma slept deeply and soundly. Co-sleeping was working out for both of them. Something else Jennifer had never imagined herself doing. 'All right, Marnie?' Jennifer said, awake suddenly.

'I think I'm in labour.'

Jennifer sat up. 'Not just Braxton-Hicks?'

'No. Getting stronger. I've been awake for hours. Judge Judy reminds me of you.'

'How so?'

'The way she thinks. She's very clear.'

'OK. Are the contractions close together?'

'Yeah. About five minutes apart now and getting stronger.'

'Have your waters broken?'

'I think so. I'm a bit damp.'

'We'd better call Willow.'

By mid-morning, Willow was ensconced in Marnie's room and all her equipment was set up, and Marnie's contractions were steady and regular. Marnie was using the gas and air during a contraction. There were two cylinders.

'Go easy on it,' Willow advised, 'if you can. Once it's gone, it's gone.' The baby's heartbeat was fine. Marnie was fine. For a while, she wandered around the house, around the garden, trying to stay mobile and upright as much as she could between contractions. But they became too much, too strong, too painful, and Marnie repaired to her bedroom. Jennifer rang Malcolm and Ethan to let them know Marnie was in labour. It felt like the right thing to do. They had both been so brilliant in the three weeks since Emma's birth. Popping round, bringing supplies, always there at the end of the phone or responding promptly to text messages. Jennifer felt she was getting into the swing of motherhood. Emma and she were finding their way. Emma was a contented baby and breastfeeding had become a little easier, less sore. Jennifer had decided to breast feed for six months. She would stop at Christmas time. In the meantime she was making sure Emma was used to bottles. It was working out, and Emma was enjoying being bottle-fed; and now that the hormones were calming down, Jennifer was enjoying motherhood. She was enjoying all it brought her – being a mother to a baby; getting to know, and to love, Marnie. The new routines, the strange sleeping patterns (or lack of patterns). It was an adventure.

At two in the afternoon, Marnie decided she couldn't stand up anymore. She crawled on to her bed. The contractions were getting longer and the space between them shorter. Willow thought the second stage was imminent. She prepared stuff, and Jennifer handed Emma over to Ethan, who had finished his McDonald's shift and popped round to see if he could help. Ethan took Emma round the garden for a walk. Willow summoned another midwife, and they stood at the end of Marnie's bed, talking quietly. Jennifer kneeled alongside Marnie, holding her hand. Marnie, stoic, brave, not making any fuss at all, steadfastly took the gas and air during the contractions. Jennifer marvelled at her daughter's courage. Jennifer has always wanted an epidural, had known she would need that absolute pain relief. Marnie had said all along that she'd want just gas and air.

At half past three, after a short but intense third stage, Marnie's baby finally slithered from her body. Jennifer gasped in shock and delight, and the midwives busied themselves, moving efficiently and speedily. Marnie cried, Jennifer kissed her, and the midwives looked at each other. Marnie reached out for her baby. Jennifer saw that the midwives were concerned. It all happened so quickly. The baby cried quietly, and Marnie pulled her to her breast, and Willow covered them both in a blanket. 'She's beautiful,' said Marnie, sobbing euphorically. She looked down at her baby, touched her face. Jennifer looked at the baby. She looked up at the midwives. Then Marnie did too. The room fell utterly silent. Perhaps no words were needed; perhaps, until the reality was stated, the reality wasn't real. Marnie pulled back the blanket and looked at her daughter closely. Then she looked again, bewildered, from Jennifer, to Willow, to the other midwife.

'Is she... is it... Down's syndrome?' Marnie asked.

Jennifer moved in closer to her daughter and her granddaughter. She put her arm firmly around Marnie's shoulders.

'I think so, yes,' said Willow.

The other midwife, older, with thick glasses, stepped forwards, and stroked Marnie's hair. 'You have a healthy and beautiful baby girl,' she said. 'All babies are unique, and they exist unto themselves. They are all imperfectly perfect, and the love in this room, and therefore this world, is all that matters. You're a strong brave young woman, and this special baby is yours because you are worthy of her. You are the one she needs. Of all the women in this world, and this is the remarkable part, you have been chosen to be her mother.'

Helena IV

'... so that's when I realised he really is a bloody idiot and not worthy of my time.'

Alison, polite, seated, watched Helena take another biscuit from the tin. It was Alison's favourite tin, and it had belonged to her mother. Alison has known this tin all of her life. She had made the biscuits early this morning, before it became too hot to bake, and she had made them for Malcolm and for Ethan. And here she was, in her own lounge, listening to this uninvited but persistent guest, say horrible things about her son. Again. Helena was right, in her own way. Ethan was a bloody idiot. But Alison was tiring of hearing it from this girl. 'Don't you think it's time you got over it?' Alison found herself saying.

Helena paused, biscuit halfway to her mouth. A steely look crept into her eyes. 'What do you mean?'

Alison panicked. She hadn't really meant to say it out loud. Mistake. Now she would have to back out of it. But— 'I mean, he let you down, yes, and he let me down, and his behaviour was unacceptable and it's resulted in a sad and sorry situation. But Ethan is my son, Helena. I love him, despite his faults.'

Helena bit on the biscuit, then spoke with her mouth full. 'He's a twat.'

It was too much. She was going too far. Alison didn't know

what to do. She took a sip of her iced tea. She watched Helena reach for a fifth biscuit.

'Actually, you've had enough of those,' Alison said. She stood, and retrieved the tin. 'I made them for Malcolm.'

'You brought them out.'

'Yes. I was being polite.'

The phone rang. Thank goodness. An awkward moment could be averted. Alison picked it up. 'Hello?'

'Mum? It's me. I'm at Jennifer's. Marnie had her baby this afternoon. But there's a problem. An issue, really. She's healthy enough and the doctor has been out to see her but she's... she's a Down's syndrome baby. They will run a few tests but it looks like she has Down's.'

Alison froze, her heart beating loud in her ears, drumming at her throat. Down's syndrome? Marnie? But wouldn't it have been more likely that Jennifer's baby would be—? 'Down's syndrome?' she said. Helena looked sharply at her.

'Yes, everybody seems to think so. It's a bit of a shock. But you should see Marnie, Mum. She's so happy. Jennifer too. I even had a cuddle and she's just a beautiful little thing. Scarlett.'

'Scarlett?' Alison saw Helena screw up her nose.

'Very Marnie-ish. Anyway, I wanted to let you know. Tell Dad, would you, please, when he gets in from work? He can come round later if he wants. You can too, of course. Always. To tell you the truth I think Jennifer could use a friend right now.'

'I see. I'm... I don't know what to say.'

'There isn't much anyone can say. It's just what's happened. Nobody's fault. We'll pull through. Little Scarlett's got her mum and Jennifer and me and Dad.'

'Yes. I'll let your dad know. Will you be home for your tea later?'

'Nah. I've offered to make something here. My McDonald's training is gonna come in useful at last. I make a mean chip.'

Alison half-laughed. Perhaps she half-sobbed. She wasn't sure. Helena was staring at her, obviously trying to piece together the conversation. She didn't want Helena to know any of it. Suddenly, she felt that. 'Take care, Ethan.'

'I will, Mum. Love you. See you later. Bye.'

Alison put the phone back in its cradle.

'What was all that about?' said Helena, finally biscuit-less.

Alison looked to the ceiling, she looked to the floor. Then she rested her gaze on the young woman sitting in Malcolm's spot on the sofa. 'Marnie has had her baby. It's a little girl and she has Down's syndrome.'

Helena laughed. 'Serves her right!'

Alison's epiphany was swift, sudden, and certain. She had no time to think, no time to dissuade herself. 'I want you to leave.'

'What?'

'Out. Now. Out of my house, out of my life, out of all our lives. Go. Ethan is not a twat. He's a young man who made a mistake, but he's doing his best. Marnie is a young woman who I think you are intensely jealous of. She's not Ethan's girlfriend any more than you are. But she needs kindness in her life and Ethan gives her that. So does Malcolm. So does Jennifer. This... this thing that's happened is not deserved by anybody. Any of them. Any of... us.'

Helena, meek, stood up. She shuffled towards the lounge door, and into the hallway, Alison following her. Helena opened the door. 'I didn't mean it,' she muttered.

'Yes, you did. You mean all the nasty little things you say. I don't want to hear them any more. Ever again. Got that?'

Malcolm's car pulled on to the drive. He got out, slowly, looking at Alison. He shut and looked the car door. The small beep of the lock felt strangely reassuring. Helena turned from Alison and brushed past Malcolm. 'She's bat shit crazy, your wife,' said Helena.

'Not really,' said Malcolm. And Helena left the garden, turned right, and was gone. Forever, Alison knew. The relief was immense.

'Everything all right?' said Malcolm, approaching her.

'You'd better come in. Ethan just rang with some worrying news.'

'What's happened?'

'I've got rid of Helena. Forever.'

'I was getting that vibe. Thank heavens, and at last. But what did Ethan say?'

'Oh, Malcolm...'

Reconciliation?

Ethan served three plates of his culinary speciality: eggs and chips. The midwives had gone. Scarlett was asleep in her mother's arms. Jennifer was changing Emma's nappy. Marnie, strong and stoic and practical, as ever, had insisted on getting up and coming downstairs. Jennifer had suggested she may prefer to stay in bed, but Marnie had thought otherwise. The midwives had helped her up. She'd had a quick shower, put on some trackies and a baggy top, and had got down the stairs with relative ease, wincing only a fraction.

Tomorrow, blood tests and hospital beckoned. But for this evening – this hot summer evening, breezeless and soft, the birds singing – peace, and plain and simple home-cooked food, and the bliss of a brand new baby, would prevail. The world had moved up, moved along, and now Scarlett was in it.

'Come and get your eggs and chips!' called Ethan. He shook salt and vinegar on to the three plates. He poured three glasses of orange juice.

Jennifer popped Emma into her bouncy chair, and wandered over to the kitchen island. 'I'll bring yours, Marnie,' she said. She put Marnie's plate on the side table next to Marnie's chair, and gave her the fork. 'Get used to eating with one hand,' said Jennifer.

'Thanks, Mum.'

Ethan's phone rang and he picked it up. After a brief call, he sat at the island and prepared to demolish his own eggs and chips. 'Dad's coming over,' he said. 'Mum let him know what's been happening.'

'Lovely,' said Jennifer.

Marnie dropped a chip on to the floor. 'Bugger!'

Jennifer picked it up. 'Five second rule,' she said, and ate it. She looked at Marnie, who was... amazing. Fresh, if that was possible. Prepared. Jennifer had no doubt she was going to sail through motherhood. Perhaps the waters would not always be calm... but Marnie would be calm. What a woman. What a daughter. Pride rose up and spilled over in Jennifer. She had never felt anything quite like it.

What had happened, in just a few months? She had gained two daughters (and more than a few pounds); she had gained a granddaughter; she had gained a new friend in Malcolm; she had a potential new friend hovering in the wings (although she wasn't at all sure anything romantic should or would ever come of it). None of this was perfect. She knew she and Marnie still had a lot to work through. She knew she still had a lot to learn about motherhood. She wasn't sure how good a grandmother she would prove to be; and she knew that while Ethan was being great now, he wouldn't always be around. He had his own life to forge, and surely complications were headed their way. All of this was real, and troubling, but it was OK.

And the losses. Jake, her protector and best boy. She'd gained Marnie, she'd lost Jake. She'd gained Malcolm, and lost Alison. Oh, Alison! Jennifer now feared that she had lost her best friend permanently. At first, she had hoped, even assumed, Alison would come round, would shed her pride. (Because pride was what it was, Jennifer knew. Sheer pride.) But now Jennifer realised there was probably – *probably* – no coming back from this. Alison was stubborn, and once her mind was made up, it was made up. Nothing much could shift her. She was hurt, and she felt betrayed. Jennifer *had* betrayed her. Sex with Ethan. Of course it wasn't right. It was rather unpleasant, really, and a mistake. An expensive mistake. So among all the gains was this terrible loss. Losing Jake was tragic, but losing Alison was... profound. Life-changing. Why did it all have to be like this? So unfair. Jennifer was wise enough to understand that this was life, this giving and taking, this balancing of the scales, these ups and downs. Nobody, not even her, had it all.

And now... beautiful Scarlett. Not a loss. Not a tragedy. But unexpected, a shock. Jennifer munched on her chips (she still had such an alarming appetite) and studied her daughters and her granddaughter. She was aware of Ethan, his plate of food already finished, scrolling on his phone.

Was this family? This feeling? These people? This moment, right now? This warmth, this contentment, this worry, this confusion, this *calm*. Not all families were calm. But this one, this newly-formed family, was calm, even among the chaos wrought by a newborn baby. Would Marnie and Scarlett stay? The honeymoon period would surely give way to a sterner reality at some point.

Both babies were fast asleep, for now, and quiet, and fed, and clean. All of them fed, and clean, and calm.

The doorbell rang.

Jennifer heard voices. Malcolm. She heard Ethan say 'Mum?!' Jennifer looked at Marnie, who shrugged, and gazed back down at her slumbering daughter. Jennifer pushed away her almost-finished plate of food, wiped her mouth, stood up. She cleared her throat. That dread feeling of apprehension and nerves had descended, and quickly. Was Alison really here?

She was. She entered the kitchen, trailing behind Ethan and Malcolm. She looked the same. It had been months since they had laid eyes on each other. Jennifer knew how different she must look – baby weight, no make-up, wearing sweat pants and a grotty old T-shirt. Hair pulled back into her long, school-style, ponytail. Very much not Jennifer.

'Hi, Alison,' she said.

'Hello, Jennifer. I... I hope... I wanted to come.'

'Of course.'

Right on cue, Emma stirred. Ethan went to her, and picked her up. He brought her over to Alison. 'This is Emma Rose. You wanna hold her?'

Alison nodded, held out her hands, let out a big sob, took her granddaughter, and laughed, and kissed the baby's forehead. 'Oh, my.'

Jennifer moved to stand alongside Alison, who continued to gaze at her granddaughter.

'Isn't she beautiful?' said Jennifer.

'She takes after her mother.'

'Oh, Alison.' Jennifer put her arm around Alison and hugged her.

Scarlett also stirred. 'This is Scarlett,' said Marnie. Alison carefully handed Emma back to Jennifer. Marnie brought Scarlett to her. 'She's pleased to meet you.'

'And I'm pleased to meet her. Another little beauty.'

'Yep,' said Jennifer. 'We know how to make gorgeous babies around here.'

Jennifer caught Ethan's eye. He shrugged, then blushed. Alison coughed a little. Marnie, seemingly oblivious, pressed Scarlett into Alison's arms. 'Hold her could you while I get a glass of water?'

'Aren't you tired, Marnie?' said Jennifer. 'Why don't you go and lie down for a while?'

'I might.'

'I should, young woman,' said Malcolm. 'You need your rest.'

Alison looked from one to the other as they spoke, Jennifer noticed. It was like their school days again: poor little Alison Baker on the periphery of everything; not quite in the gang. Jennifer had stepped in then, and she would step in now. 'Alison, are you all right holding Scarlett while I help Marnie tidy up her bed? It needs clean stuff.'

'Of course,' said Alison.

Scarlett started to wail. 'She's hungry,' said Marnie.

'In that case,' Jennifer said, 'you feed her, and let me and Alison get your room ready.'

'Sure.' Marnie took Scarlett from Alison. 'Put Emma back in her bouncy chair,' Marnie said. 'I'll keep an eye on her.'

'Well,' said Malcolm. 'As we are all here, why don't Ethan and I go and buy a nice bottle of champagne so we can welcome little Scarlett into the world properly?'

'No need,' said Jennifer. 'I've two bottles in the fridge already. Bought them for Emma but we never got round to opening them. We could do with some fancy nibbles, though. Come on, Alison. Let's go and make that bed up.'

Marnie's room was, predictably, Alison thought, a mess. Not just post-giving-birth mess, although that was in evidence. It was pure chaos. Clothes spilling from the wardrobe and the chest of drawers. The dressing table covered in bottles, tubes, cans, dust. Piles of clothes were scattered across the floor; whether clean or dirty Alison guessed even Marnie didn't know. 'My goodness,' said Alison, hands on hips, surveying the room.

'She's not like me,' said Jennifer.

'She is, in many ways.'

'Is she?'

'Why didn't you ever tell me about her?'

Jennifer stripped the bed linen from the bed. 'I didn't tell anybody. I didn't want anyone trying to persuade me one way or the other.'

'When Ethan was born you pretended to know nothing about childbirth.'

'Yes.'

'That must have been a lonely experience.'

'It was rather, yes.'

'Let me take all that downstairs.'

'Let's just gather up anything and everything that looks like laundry and I'll get it all washed for her.'

'Good idea.'

Jennifer and Alison each gathered up and then carried a huge pile of linen and clothing downstairs, and dumped it all on the kitchen floor by the washing machine. Marnie was peacefully feeding Scarlett. Emma was quietly bouncing. Jennifer grabbed her handheld vacuum cleaner from its charge point and the two women returned to Marnie's room.

In no time it was neat enough, with fresh bed linen. Jennifer positioned a Moses basket alongside the bed. 'I bought two of these,' she said.

'Good idea.'

'My life has taken rather a turn.'

'Hasn't it just.'

They sat alongside each other on the bed. 'I'm sorry,' said Jennifer.

'For what?'

'Seducing Ethan. It was ridiculous. It should never have happened.'

'Right. But it did. And now you have a baby.'

'Yes.'

'So something good has come from quite a... sordid situation. Look, Jennifer. I won't ever pretend to be happy about what happened. I took it very hard.'

'I know.'

'But I overreacted. Perhaps wrongly reacted would be more accurate.'

'Not really. You had every right to—'

'Let me finish. Please.'

'OK.'

'I know the kind of woman you are, Jennifer.'

'Was.'

'Whatever. You love men, and they love you. You're sexy, even now.'

Jennifer laughed ruefully and looked at her sweat pants, her scruffy T-shirt.

'No, I mean it. You have sex appeal in spades and I don't. I suppose I've always been a little jealous of you.'

'I was jealous of you. When Ethan was born.'

'I did wonder, at the time. And you became very distant.'

'I didn't exactly regret giving up Marnie, but I wished I'd been a better woman. More mumsy.'

'And now look at you!'

'I know. Crazy, isn't it?'

'Its rather... wonderful.'

'Is it?'

'Your grown-up daughter returned to you, a new baby daughter, a granddaughter. I too have a granddaughter... Little Scarlett... will she need tests?'

'Yes. We are taking her to hospital tomorrow.'

'It's a shock.'

'It should have been my baby.'

'I'm so glad it wasn't. But I do feel for Marnie.'

'We all do.'

'But Marnie is... she's strong, isn't she? She'll fight Scarlett's corner.'

'We both will.'

'We *all* will.'

'Thank you, Ally.'

Alison nodded. 'And I will... try to... overlook things.'

Relief flooded through Jennifer. But: 'Overlook isn't quite right though, is it? The parentage of Emma can't really be overlooked.'

'Accepted, then. Got over.'

'That was my thinking.'

'I promise to get over it. In my own time. I will, you know. I'm not as prudish as you think.'

'Oh, I know that!'

Alison lowered her voice: 'You're thinking of Danny Boy?'

'Might be.'

'Malcolm knows all about it.'

'How?'

'I've no idea. Did you tell him?'

Jennifer gave Alison a very Jennifer look.

'OK, OK, sorry. Of course you didn't.'

'Correct. I'd never... but how on earth did he find out?'

'I guess we'll never know. It came out in a row. I don't think we'll ever discuss it again, but he knew.'

'Wait. You and Malc had a row?'

'Yes. Our first one. We never row.'

'I know.'

'But maybe we should. It seemed to clear the air. And I dumped Helena.'

'*The* Helena?'

'She was there when Ethan rang and she said... it doesn't matter what she said, but it was unkind and I told her to leave.'

'She was never good enough for Ethan.'

'Absolutely not. Not good enough for me, either.'

'Well done, Ally Pally.'

'Do you mind if I ask you to stop calling me that?'

'Sorry.'

'It makes me feel inferior. Like I'm your little lap dog or something.'

'I am sorry, Alison. It was thoughtless of me to keep using it after our school years.'

'It was, yes.'

They sat in silence, considering all the new avenues opening up between them. The shifts, the new ways, the admissions. It was... refreshing.

'I'm sorry about Jake,' said Alison. 'Genuinely. I know how much you loved that boy of yours.'

Jennifer put her hand out. Alison took it.

'I'm heartbroken, really,' said Jennifer. 'I mean, Jake was a dog, not a human, and certainly not a baby, but I still feel it. I feel his absence and I hate it. He was like a friend to me. He *was* a friend to me.'

'One of your... few friends?'

'One of two, Alison. And I lost them both over the course of this strange summer.'

'I think you may get one back. If you want her.'

Jennifer pulled Alison to her, and they hugged, hard and long, silently.

When they heard Malcolm and Ethan return, with, hopefully, fancy nibbles, they leaped up from the bed, and wiped their faces, and laughed at each other.

'What are we like?' said Alison.

'I hope we are like friends,' said Jennifer.

'I think we might be.'

'Let's go open those beautiful bottles of champagne,' said

Jennifer, and she took Alison's hand. It felt warm and comforting.

'Let's do that,' said Alison, smiling, and together they went downstairs.

AUTUMN

The Phone Calls IV and V

'Marnie, you want a peppermint tea?'

'Green tea, please!'

Jennifer flicked the kettle on. She wandered to the French windows and pulled back the curtains. The garden was white with frost, the first of the season. Spider webs were draped across the bare plants. Birds hopped around on the lawn and on the feeders. She must top them up today.

'Toast too, love?' Jennifer called, opening the bread bin.

Marnie wandered in, carrying Scarlett. 'I will if you will,' she said.

'Why not? White-bread-toast-with-jam?' If a year ago Jennifer had been told she would be eating such foodstuffs, she would never have believed it. But here she was, white bread and jam agogo. But she was careful. Once a week, if that. She had lost a few pounds and wanted to keep them off. Not that it seemed to matter too much any more. She couldn't recall the last time she'd worn any of her high heeled shoes. "Imelda", Alison had once called her. Maybe it was time for a sort-out and a trip, or several, to the charity shops. "Imelda" seemed to have left the building. Jennifer quite liked the new woman who had taken her place.

Marnie flumped down on to the sofa and surveyed the frosty garden. 'That summer seems a long time ago now.'

'Doesn't it! And what a summer it was. But I'm glad, really, that it's over. It got too hot.'

'Can summer ever be too hot?'

'Yes! When you're heavily pregnant, yes.'

'You're probably right. It did get a bit warm. I loved sleeping down here though.' It had become so hot in the days following Scarlett's birth that Marnie had decamped to the kitchen-diner, dragging her mattress downstairs and sleeping with her baby by the open French windows. Jennifer had not been entirely comfortable with it.

Intruders, Marnie?

What's the chances?

I wish we still had Jake...

I'm sorry, Mum.

I've told you a million times, it wasn't your fault. I'm not mad at you.

Anymore...

Yes. That's right. I'm not mad at you anymore.

Shall we get a new dog?

I don't know, Marnie. It's too soon.

Let's think about it next year?

Deal. Now it looks like our girls are getting hungry...

The hungry girls were growing. Emma was now a bundle of podge. She was smiling, gurgling, laughing, grabbing things. She was also trying to roll over and Jennifer sensed it would be any day now. She was going to be an early developer. Like mother, like daughter. Jennifer pushed that thought away and finished preparing the peppermint tea in her peppermint tea pot. A "new mother" gift from Alison last week for Jennifer. She'd found it in a charity shop. It was a pretty tea pot, floral, with lots of pink and green. Just right for peppermint tea. She and Marnie had developed a taste for it after the girls were born. Iced mint tea initially, then as the extraordinary summer finally subsided in September, they took it hot and strong. It was a thoughtful gift.

Jennifer's mobile rang just as she had finished feeding Emma. She didn't recognise the number, but she tended to pick up unknown callers these days. It could be their GP (still young and funky, and a great doctor, and very involved with Scarlett), the hospital, the health visitor. 'Jennifer Sawyer.'

'Hi, Jennifer. It's Adam.'

'Adam?'

Marnie's head jerked up. 'Adam?' she mouthed.

'Hi... Adam. Hi.'

'I lost my old phone and had to get a new one. Luckily I'm an old-fashioned chap and still write numbers down. The important ones, anyway.' He paused for effect.

Jennifer smiled. 'Wicked,' she said, borrowing one of Marnie's most-favoured words.

'Oh, God. That was so corny, wasn't it?' Adam said.

'Yes.'

'Let me start again. How is everybody?'

Jennifer filled him in on the latest developments, the babies' milestones...

Surely Adam would be bored...? But he listened attentively, and asked intelligent questions. He seemed very pleased when she told him she and Alison were "back on".

'That's great, Jen. Really.'

Jen? Since when? Should she correct—? No. It was OK. It was rather nice, really. Nobody had ever called her Jen. She had never allowed anybody to. But from Adam, it sounded, and felt... easy. Right. She would allow it.

'It is rather nice. She took me out for afternoon tea last week. We chatted away like no tomorrow and it was just like

225

old times. Actually, that's not quite true. It was like new and improved times.'

'Sounds great.'

The ensuing pause was not uncomfortable. Then Adam said, 'Would you like that dinner with me? Sometime? Soon, maybe? If you feel... if you'd like to.'

'You want a date with a woman who had a baby four months ago, is still breastfeeding, weighs a few more pounds than she used to, can't recall the last time she put on her make-up, and slobs around in elastic-waisted slacks day and night?'

'Yes.'

This time the silence was a little more uncomfortable. That was a very serious Yes. No equivocation. He was breathing quickly. Nervously, she realised. 'OK.'

'OK to what?'

'Dinner.'

'Really?'

'Yes,' said Jennifer.

'Name a day.'

'Are you free on Saturday?'

'I am, absolutely.'

Arrangements were made. He would pick her up. Marnie, feeding Scarlett, looking on for the duration of the conversation, thoroughly entertained.

'What?' said Jennifer after she finished the call.

'Nothing.'

'It's just a simple date. Friendly. Not romantic.'

'He *is* quite good-looking, in his own way.'

'I know that, Marnie.'

Marnie chuckled.

'What?'

'Nothing. I'll babysit. I wondered... I thought, if you are OK with it, I can feed Emma too if you like. Sometimes. My milk.'

'Oh! I don't know. Will it interfere with your supply?'

'In a good way. It will help me make more. I wanna breastfeed Scarlett until she's a year old.'

'Good for you. That should be OK. Convenient, I suppose? But I don't think I'll manage a year. I'm thinking of introducing formula soon.'

'Uh-huh.'

'Marnie! Not for those sort of reasons.'

'*What* sort of reasons?'

'I know what you're thinking. Adam and me and being... intimate.'

'I was not thinking that!'

'Whatever. We won't be getting intimate. I'm through with all romantic notions where men are concerned. I told you, he is a friend.'

'A good-looking one.'

'Haven't we had this conversation already?'

Marnie put Scarlett over her shoulder. 'Just have fun, Mum. OK? You deserve it. Sex or not, have fun.'

'Thanks. I intend to. I think.'

Jennifer's phone rang again. 'Jennifer Sawyer.'

'Hello, Jennifer Sawyer.'

'Alison! You all right?'

'Yes, thank you, I am. Ethan has got a job. A proper job. He's handed in his notice at McDonald's.'

'What's he going to be doing?'

'Some sort of IT support thingy for one of the banks in town. Actually for all the branches within quite a sizeable radius.'

'It's lucky he passed his driving test then.'

'Yes. Thanks again for all your help.'

'It's not a problem, Alison. I just want this whole... situation... to work out. For all of us. For Emma. You know?'

'I do know, Jennifer. Really I do.'

'It's still very nice to hear your voice.'

She had never spoken like this to Alison. Not once. And that had been remiss of her, all these years. Taking Alison for granted, assuming she would always be "there", hovering in the background of her life.

'Oh,' said Alison. 'Ditto.'

'You do know you are my best friend, don't you? And Malc too, actually. You are my friends. The closet thing I've ever had to a family, really, in my adulthood.'

'That's... nice, Jennifer. Thank you.'

'And I know I've been a complete bitch over the years. Selfish and thoughtless.'

'We all have our moments.'

'I know. But I had too many where you're concerned. I took you for granted.'

'Perhaps you did, a bit.'

'Not any more, I promise. I want us to get back to what we once were, or maybe what we never truly were. Where we should have been. Do you know what I mean?'

'I think so. Anyway, how is my granddaughter today?'

'Oh she is splendid, Granny.'

'Nan.'

'Granny.'

'Are we arguing?'

Jennifer paused, smiled to herself. 'No, we're not arguing, Nan.'

Jennifer had financed Ethan's driving lessons and bought a car for him. A nice little second-hand dark blue Honda Jazz, nothing fancy. With a black box fitted. Not that it was needed: Ethan was Malcolm's son when it came to driving. Jennifer knew that the ability to drive would be useful, if not necessary, for Ethan's future as an active and involved father of his little girl; and *young Ethan may as well start being useful now.* Plus he needed a good job, and now he had one. He'd talked of putting a bit of money by every month for Emma. Jennifer, appreciative of the sentiment, had assured him it wasn't necessary. 'Just get a career up and running,' she'd said. *First things first, Ethan.*

That Dinner

Adam arrived promptly at half past seven. He had booked a table for eight. It was a mild November evening, dry, still. Rather a pity he had decided to drive, she thought. They could have walked and shared a bottle of wine.

Jennifer fussed around Emma – and Scarlett, and Marnie – before leaving.

Marnie sighed and rolled her eyes at Adam. 'For goodness sake, Mum, just go and have your night out. I'm fine, Scarlett's fine, and Emma's fine.'

'All right. I know. I'm sorry. I'm ready, Adam, if you are?'

'Let's go.'

She wasn't sure how he had got a table, but twenty minutes later they were seated in a small, private alcove in *Le Manoir Elegante*. A very famous restaurant in the middle of nowhere, five miles or so out of town: exclusive, expensive, and classy. The waiting list for a table was a year, so she'd heard. Ally had been banging on about— *Alison* had been talking about it, once. Half-considering booking a table for her and Malcolm for their anniversary last year, then discovering she was far too late. That's why they had made do with Mario's. But it wasn't really making do because Mario's was a lovely place to eat. So said Alison. She and Malcolm had dined there again this year on their anniversary. But the dinner had been strained, a bit quiet. Alison said, looking back now, she hadn't quite realised how Malcolm had become so stressed and upset with all that had gone on... the rift, the poisonous presence of Helena. He was much happier now.

The table was covered in thick white linen, the white candle in the middle of the table in a crystal vase was fresh and newly lighted. The cutlery and glasses gleamed. The waiter was named Gerard and was excessively polite. Jennifer wasn't entirely comfortable in this environment, but just a year ago, she would have been. It was the kind of place she'd half-hoped Simon might have taken her to, but he never did. But now this restaurant felt pretentious. What on earth had happened to her? Babies, that's what. Motherhood had finally caught up with her, and with it came a new person, a new life, a new set of priorities. Honestly, any pub in town would have sufficed. Burger and chips. A glass of cheap plonk.

But Adam had obviously decided only the poshest restaurant around was good enough for their first date. If it was a date. Jennifer wasn't sure. It was sort-of-a-date, and sort-of-not. She wasn't in date mode. Better get that across to Adam, and fast, before he got any ideas. She didn't intend kissing him tonight, let alone anything else.

'Adam, I—'

'It's all right, Jen. I think I know what you're going to say.'

The waiter had poured the wine. They had ordered their food. The restaurant buzzed quietly with chatter and ambience.

'You do?'

'I think so. You are not ready for a full-blown dating situation. You want to be friends. You are wondering why I've brought you here and you feel a little uncomfortable.'

'Wow. You're very perceptive.'

'Yes, I am.'

Jennifer took a sip of the expensive wine.

'Truth is, Jennifer, I like you, very much. You are an attractive woman, and you're astute and intelligent.'

'Oh. Thank you. Keep talking!'

'And I want your opinion on something.'

'All right.'

'You like it here?'

She explained how she felt. He listened intently. 'Why do you want my opinion, anyway?' she asked.

'I just wanted to know how you like it. I guess you must have eaten here before?'

'Funnily enough, I haven't.'

'That is quite surprising.'

'Perhaps.'

'So do you like it?'

'It's fine. I probably would have liked it more last year...'

'Yes. I get what you're saying. But in general it's highly regarded, no? It's an occasion, to eat here? People eat here *on* occasions?'

'Oh, yes.'

She sipped her wine. What was he getting at?

'Richard and I are thinking of buying it,' said Adam. 'We— *I* wanted a second opinion.'

Jennifer took a large gulp of wine.

WINTER

No More Shocks

Marnie woke first on Christmas morning. She went downstairs to make tea for them both, and to put on the oven to start the turkey. They were expecting three guests for dinner, and including the babies, there would be seven around the table. Luckily Jennifer had a large table in her rarely-used dining room.

Jennifer heard the kettle boiling. She heard the living room door open. She heard a small cry of delight.

A few minutes later Marnie entered Jennifer's bedroom with the tea tray – green tea for both of them – and a Christmas stocking bulging with gifts.

'Mum!' cried Marnie. 'I didn't do one for you!'

'And quite right too.'

'Can I open it now?'

'Of course. Let's enjoy the peace before the girls wake up. And think about it: next year we are bound to be awoken by a very excited Emma and Scarlett...'

'I s'pose we will, won't we?'

Jennifer nodded sagely.

Marnie pulled out from her stocking Lush products, vegan make-up, a fancy copy of *The Bell Jar*. A satsuma, an apple, a walnut, a Brazil nut, and a hazelnut. She exclaimed over it all, her face flushed, animated. Jennifer sipped her tea and suppressed her tears. This could have – should have – happened twenty-three times already. But it was their first Christmas. And not their last. And it was OK. This was the thought she tried to keep in her mind. It was all going to be OK.

Marnie was making the vegan stuffing. Jennifer was pretty sure all stuffings were vegan, but decided to say nothing. What was the point? It was a privilege to be enjoying their first Christmas together and although they often clashed in the kitchen, Jennifer was determined that wouldn't happen today. The turkey was in the large oven in her Rangemaster; Marnie's root vegetable tarte Tatin in the smaller one. Marnie was proving to be a great cook, and Jennifer found that she was enjoying many of her vegan dishes. So much so that she had suggested a couple of them to Adam and Richard for *Le Manoir Elegante*. Whether they would pass the ideas on to their newly-hired and very prestigious Australian chef was another matter. Jennifer was looking forward to finding out. The re-opening was planned for March. Jennifer and Marnie were both invited to attend, as the Godden brothers' special guests.

Of course, she missed Jake; her first Christmas without him since his arrival in her life as a bouncing playful puppy. Early on Christmas Day she used to take him for a long walk, then spoil him rotten for the rest of the morning before she left him to go round to Alison's for dinner. Jake had loved pigs in blankets.

How strange life was. How it gave and took away at the same time. How it went in and out of tune, harmony, and key. The impermanence of life was not something she had ever really given any thought to, and perhaps that was something to be a little ashamed of. She had been too shallow, too often, throughout her life, so far. Yet she found herself thinking about mortality this day: Christmas Day, with its regularity, its customs, its trappings and trimmings, was perhaps the most immortal day of the year. She felt *safe* on Christmas Day – cosy, cossetted, immune… even on those Christmas Days she had spent with Patrick… and perhaps she felt safer on this one than any before. She had two daughters, and a granddaughter, all of them "bonny" (Alison's word) and well and healthy, under her roof, in her care. It was going to be the best Christmas she had ever known. Her only regret was that Jake was not here to enjoy it with them. Instead he was under the ground, alongside her house, nourishing her wild garden, which she knew would come into its own in the summer. It was something to look forward to, and she was glad her darling Jake would still be making his presence felt.

At half past eleven, the doorbell rang.

'I'll go!' called Marnie. Jennifer was upstairs changing Emma's nappy, and attempting to dress her in a little Santa-style frock she had bought for her. Emma was a wriggler. And, Jennifer suspected, even now, not a fan of wearing frocks.

Jennifer heard the guests' cheerful greetings, as jolly as carol singers, as she shoved Emma's chubby little arm into a sleeve. 'Come on, little lady,' she said. 'Your dad can entertain you for a while!'

Ethan was glad to do so, and carried Emma off to her toys, and got down on the floor with her. He was good at playing with Emma, and Jennifer wasn't. It was a skill she felt she couldn't develop, so she left it for Ethan. It worked.

Jennifer hugged Malcolm, and dragged Alison over to the fridge, which she opened. 'Champagne or Baileys?' Jennifer asked.

Alison contemplated the bottles. 'Let's have a Baileys now, and champagne with dinner.'

'Good idea, as ever, young Alison. Grab some ice from the dispenser, would you please, and I'll pour.'

Jennifer poured a generous Baileys for each of them. She had beers too for Malcolm and Ethan, and a nice vegan white wine for Marnie, and soon all the grown-ups were enjoying the first drink of Christmas Day.

'Is there anything I can do to help?' asked Alison, leaning on the kitchen island.

'No, I think it's all under control. Marnie, bless her, got up and popped the oven on for the turkey first thing. Everything else is prepped and just needs shoving in the ovens at the right time.'

'Gosh. You have become quite the domestic goddess!'

'Oh no, I haven't. I really haven't. Marnie's the cook, I can assure you.'

'Maybe so, but look at you... school m'am frock and pinny and slippers!'

Jennifer shrugged. 'There isn't much room for glamour in my life these days.'

'Do you mind that?'

'No. Funnily enough, I don't. I really don't. It all feels... right, you know?'

'Yeah, I know. And how are you and Adam getting on?'

'Fine.'

Alison waited, raising her eyebrows.

'Fine. That's all. We are friends, and so far, nothing more. I like it.'

'He's very handsome. In his unique way.'

'So everybody keeps reminding me.'

'It's hard not to notice.'

'Yet somehow, I don't. His looks feel immaterial.'

Alison smiled, a broad grin. 'Well, well, well. A platonic friendship at last!'

'I wouldn't go that far, Alison.'

'Ah... so it's not quite platonic, then?'

Jennifer opened the oven door and lifted out the turkey. 'Ninety-five per cent platonic. We *have* kissed.'

Alison whispered, 'I can't blame you for that.'

'Could you come and baste the turkey, please? I need to nip to the loo.'

'Of course. How's the restaurant purchase going?'

'All right, I think. It's already bought. They're now preparing for the re-opening. Re-branding, really, in many ways. They're hired this hotshot chef from Australia.'

'Ethan mentioned that to me. Sounds like they have Plans.'

'Oh, they've got Plans all right. Back in a mo.'

Jennifer reappeared a couple of minutes later, bearing a small parcel, beautifully wrapped. 'This is for you,' she said. 'I wanted to give it to you now so nobody else sees. I mean, you can show Malcolm later. But I wanted it to be... private.'

'What on earth is it?'

'Open it and see. Quick!'

'Turkey's basted.'

'Thanks. I'll pop it back in.'

Alison opened her present. Her face reddened, then brightened, then she beamed. 'Oh, Jennifer!'

It was a beautiful silver locket, with a diamond set in the front, and inside there was a tiny photo each of Ethan and Emma.

'I thought it a bit... flashy,' said Jennifer. 'Didn't want to show off.'

'Don't be silly. It's beautiful, not flashy. Here, help me put it on.'

Jennifer did up the clasp, Alison turned, and Jennifer admired the locket. 'Lovely!' she said. 'Put it back in the box.'

Alison beamed. 'If I must. Thank you. It's a beautiful gift.'

'For my beautiful friend.'

'Oh, shut up.'

They paused, both knowing they wanted to say something, but not quite sure what, or how to say it. Things had been cordial; warm, even, at times, since their reconciliation. Alison had been nothing less than a doting grandmother to Emma, and also showed Scarlett a great deal of affection and attention. But somehow their friendship – their new-look friendship – wasn't quite complete. They weren't back to normal... and both suspected they never would be.

'Alison, I—'

'No. Let me. Please.' Alison pushed back her hair, and took off her new locket. 'I know things haven't been easy this past year.'

'I know that too.'

'And I also know that some of it was my fault. Not all of it, but much of it.'

'And much of it was my fault.'

'Yes. But maybe we need to move away from the concept of fault and blame. It doesn't help either of us. Any of us, actually.'

'OK.'

'What matters is Emma. None of this is her fault, that's for sure. She finds herself in this world, in this family. We all owe her the love she deserves.'

'Yes.'

'And Scarlett too, bless her. And Marnie, come to that. And Ethan. Four kids who need us.'

'This is what I've been thinking.'

'And I know we are friends again and thank heavens... but it's more than that now, isn't it? Our relationship?'

'Y...e...s...'

'Damn it, Jennifer! Will you never stop being infuriating?'

'I'm sorry. I don't mean to be. Go on.'

'What I'm trying to say, in my no doubt hopelessly "Alison" way, is that we... we're... we are family.'

Jennifer felt hot tears form. Alison saw them. 'Jennifer?'

'Yes?'

'Our friendship feels different because it *is* different. We're on a different footing now, and I like it. It's better. You don't get to choose your family.'

'No.'

'You're Emma's mum and Ethan's her dad and I'm her nan, Malcolm's her granddad. We're her family.'

Jennifer gave in to the tears and covered her eyes. Alison took a step towards her and flung her arms around her. 'It's OK,' said Alison. 'It's all going to be OK.'

'After my mum and then my dad died I felt... family-less. Patrick was no husband. Jake was my family, my only family. I should've... I should've been a better friend to you, Alison.'

'And so should I to you. We don't always see eye-to-eye, we never have, and that's fine. It's healthy, isn't it? And yes we've had our ups and downs... but look at us now.'

Jennifer sniffed, and wiped her eyes with her pinny. 'Yeah. Look at us now.'

'That's the spirit.'

And it was. Dinner went like a dream. Alison loved the root vegetable tarte Tatin. She wasn't a vegan, of course, but she enjoyed vegan food from time to time. Marnie looked half-pleased, half-irritated, but she smiled sweetly. *Part-time vegans missed the obvious point,* she had often complained to Jennifer. Jennifer had asked for, insisted on, a Christmas Day food-truce. 'Our guests will eat what they like, and you and I will accept that with good grace,' Jennifer had said. Marnie had agreed.

Malcolm poured more champagne once the glasses, and plates, were empty, and they discussed preparing and eating dessert later. It was agreed that Jennifer and Marnie would serve desserts after the queen's speech. Alison watched it every year, and so it was going to be on Jennifer's television. Marnie said she would change the babies' nappies, or something, while the speech was on.

They pulled their crackers, read out the jokes, put on the silly hats. The doorbell rang. Marnie looked at Jennifer, Jennifer looked at Marnie. 'I'll go!' cried Marnie cheerfully.

Adam wandered into the dining room. Marnie following him. He was carrying a beautifully-wrapped gift. Jennifer stood up. 'Adam?!'

'I'm sorry. I'm interrupting.'

'No. No, not at all,' said Jennifer. She felt her face redden and knew that Alison was scrutinising her.

'Everybody, this is my friend, Adam. Adam, meet Alison, her husband Malcolm, and their son Ethan.'

Greetings ensued, and Malcolm offered Adam a glass of champagne.

'Oh no, thank you. I'm driving. And I can't stay, I'm due at my brother's for dinner about twenty minutes ago. Listen, Jennifer, this is for you.' He handed over the gift. 'And I have what might be a good proposition for you.' Adam pulled out a chair alongside Ethan. 'So, how are you finding being a dad?'

'Interesting,' said Ethan.

'I bet,' said Adam.

'I'm very proud too.'

'Of course. I don't have kids, but I can imagine the feelings.'

'It makes life very... different.'

'Yes, it must be wild. So,' said Adam, turning to Jennifer. 'I actually came round to talk to you about... well, a friend of a friend has a dog they can no longer take care of. Health reasons, that's all. The dog is fine. She has a great temperament, and she needs a home.'

'What breed?' asked Jennifer.

'Get this. She's a golden shepherd.'

'Perfect for Christmas Day then!' said Alison. She was getting tipsy.

'Alison, yes. I thought so too,' said Adam. 'What do you think, Jen?'

'Jen?' said Alison. 'Blimey, Adam, you are honoured!'

'Alison...' said Malcolm quietly.

'It's all right, Malc,' said Jennifer. 'I just haven't got round to telling Adam yet how I hate being called Jen or Jenny.'

Adam turned red. 'Really?'

'Mostly, yes, really. But from you... I'll allow it.'

'Phew.'

Alison raised her eyebrows, but said nothing.

'How old is this golden shepherd?' asked Jennifer.

'Two and a half years.'

'Does she have a name?'

'Oh, yes.'

'And...?'

'Her name is Emma. Believe it or not.'

Marnie said, 'It's meant to be then!'

'If you like,' said Adam, 'we could – you could – go and visit, maybe after the new year? See if you like this dog. She is really beautiful.'

'That sounds great, Adam,' said Jennifer. 'Thank you. No promises though. I'm not sure I'm ready to replace Jake. And the babies keep us both so busy.'

'I wanted to give you a heads-up. I have to go. I'm spending the rest of the day with Rich and his new lady-friend. I'll call you, and we'll arrange a visit to go see Emma in the new year.'

Adam left to a chorus of goodbyes. Jennifer saw him out.

'Emz,' she said.

Adam opened the front door. 'What?'

'Emz. That's what we'll call the dog. Or that's what we'll call Emma. One of them will be Emz.'

Adam smiled, and Jennifer reached out, pulled him to her, and kissed him.

Eventually, Adam extricated himself. 'Oh, heck, I really do have to go,' he said.

'I know. It's fine. Catch up in a few days?'

'Absolutely. It was nice to meet your friends. They're a great bunch.'

'Oh, they are. Truly good people, too. But they're not my friends. They're my family.'

AUTHOR & PUBLISHER NOTE

I need to thank all the self-publishing authors who have inspired me, and helped me to become a better writer, author, and publisher. There are some truly talented and inventive "authorpreneurs" out there who are professional, dedicated, and knowledgeable.

If you have enjoyed this book, and even if you haven't, I would be very grateful for on-line reviews. Reviews are the life-blood of books, helping to make them more visible throughout the book trade. Even one sentence counts as a review. Thanks!

You can find out more about me, my former indie press, and my books on my website: louisewaltersbooks.co.uk.

And you can find me ranting, raving, or just saying stuff quietly, on Twitter: LouiseWalters12.

Louise

2024

LWB SUPPORTERS

All the people listed here took out subscriptions at my indie press and in doing so helped me enormously as a publisher. I'm forever grateful to them for their support of my press and my authors' books.

Heartfelt thanks to:

Claire Allen
Edie Anderson
Karen Ankers
Francesca Bailey-Karel
Tricia Beckett
JEJ Bray
Melanie Brennan
Tom & Sue Carmichael
Liz Carr
Penny Carter-Francis
Pippa Chappell
Eric Clarke
Louise Cook
Deborah Cooper
Tina deBellegarde
Giselle Delsol

James Downs
Jill Doyle
Kathryn Eastman
Melissa Everleigh
Rowena Fishwick
Harriet Freeman
Diane Gardner
Ian Hagues
Andrea Harman
Stephanie Heimer
Debra Hills
Karen Hilton
Henrike Hirsce
Claire Hitch
Amanda Huggins
Cath Humphris
Christine Ince
Julie Irwin
Merith Jones
Seamus Keaveny
Moon Kestrel
Ania Kierczyńska
Anne Lindsay
Michael Lynes
Karen Mace
Anne Maguire
Marie-Anne Mancio
Karen May
Cheryl Mayo
Jennifer McNicol
MoMoBookDiary
Rosemary Morgan
Jackie Morrison

Louise Mumford
Trevor Newton
Aveline Perez de Vera
Mary Picken
Helen Poore
Helen Poyer
Clare Rhoden
Rebecca Shaw
Gillian Stern
John Taylor
Julie Teckman
Sarah Thomas
Sue Thomas
Mark Thornton
Penny Tofiluk
Mary Turner
Ian Walters
Steve Walters
Charles Waterhouse
Elizabeth Waugh
Alexis Wolfe
Finola Woodhouse
Louise Wykes